A PILGRIM SHADOW

A PILGRIM SHADOW

ALAN C. HUFFINES

EAKIN PRESS ⬥ Austin, Texas

Cover photograph, from left to right: George, Boone, Alfred, Lewellyn, and Charley Marlow. Image taken circa 1881 in Fort Sill, Indian Territory. Courtesy Marlow Chamber of Commerce, Marlow, Oklahoma.

Map page vi courtesy Bill Stone.

Library of Congress Cataloging-in-Publication Data

Huffines, Alan C.
  A pilgrim shadow / Alan Huffines.–1st ed.
    p. cm.
  ISBN 1-57168-529-4
    1. Texas–History–1846-1950–Fiction. 2. Young County (Tex.)–Fiction. 3. Marlow family–Fiction. I. Title.
PS3608.U55 P55 2001
813'.54–dc21
                    2001040461

FIRST EDITION
Copyright © 2001 by Alan C. Huffines
Published in the U.S.A.
By Eakin Press
A Division of Sunbelt Media, Inc.
P.O. Drawer 90159
Austin, Texas 78709-0159
email: eakinpub@sig.net
website: www.eakinpress.com

ELDORADO

Gaily bedight
A gallant knight
In sunshine and in shadow
Had journeyed long,
Singing a song
In search of Eldorado

But he grew old-
This knight so bold-
And o'er his heart a shadow
Fell as he found
No spot of ground
That looked like Eldorado

And, as his strength
Failed him at length,
He met a pilgrim shadow-
"Shadow," said he,
"Where can it be-
This land of Eldorado?"

"Over the Mountains
Of the Moon,
Down the Valley of the Shadow,
Ride, boldly ride,"
The shade replied-
"If you seek for Eldorado!"

—EDGAR ALLEN POE

Dedicated to the

Glory of God

And for the ladies in my life:

Caroline, Morgan, Madison, and Melissa

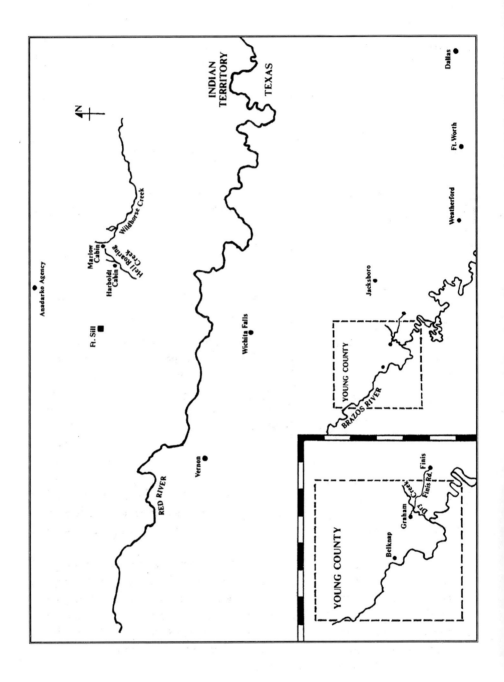

PROLOGUE

This is the first time in the annals of history where unarmed prisoners, shackled together, ever repelled a mob. Such cool courage that preferred to fight... and die... in glorious battle rather than... ignominiously by a frenzied mob, desires to be commemorated in song and story.
—FEDERAL JUDGE A. P. McCORMICK

In 1877 leading stock barons from twenty-seven North and West Texas counties formed the Texas Cattle Raisers Association. They organized under a tree in Graham that, since 1936, bears a Texas State Historical Marker recognizing the fact. Those cattle "barons" were the significant economic and political force in Texas following the Civil War, and Young County, Texas, served as their geographic center. The barons not only held most of the land and controlled the economy, they employed small armies to do their bidding. The late nineteenth century on the Texas frontier was a feudal time reminiscent of the Middle Ages, with cattle barons analogous to the great landholders of Europe. When the barons could not force their hand with their own means, they subcontracted with the law. In 1888 a U.S. marshal was paid only in rewards and a per diem of about six cents a mile when he had warrants and was in pursuit. To supplement this allowance, the barons paid some marshals $150 per month, ensuring that their interests were accomplished.

Often, much of the barons' herds and remudas ran on open range north of the Red River in the Indian Territory (IT). Rustling had always been the bane of the barons, and this was especially true with the generally unsupervised herds in the territory. Young County, Texas, was the seat of federal government for a large portion of the IT and held the northernmost law enforcement and judiciary to stem the problem.

The following is a true story.

PART I

AUGUST–SEPTEMBER 1888

CHAPTER 1

SUN BOY'S RANCH
INDIAN TERRITORY

The horses were screaming. It was not the scream of a woman or a catamount, but it was as terrible to hear. Two dozen horse colts had their front legs hobbled and were suspended by their tails beneath a series of long cross-timbers and uprights. There were two colts to each crossbar. August was castration time on the ranch. The cowboys had spent most of the month rounding up the brood mares and their offspring. Some of the remuda had been as far away as the Wichita Mountains, the other side of Fort Sill. Once located by the drovers working in pairs, the animals were driven into a series of catch corrals and traps. Why they did not castrate then and there was curious, but Chief Sun Boy wanted the castings at the ranch headquarters, or "lodge" as he called it. The chief never accompanied the roundups. Mounted whites with guns made him nervous, he said. It was the ranch joke. There were whites, but fully one-third of the cowboys employed by the chief were Indians, Negroes, or Mexicans.

The casting crew worked efficiently. The lead, or number one, man gave each colt two scrotum incisions and was closely followed by the number two man, who pulled the testicles free. The incisions were the delicate issue. All of the men were well trained at castrating calves, which only required cutting loose the scrotum. Horses could not be cut straight line. The lead man making the cut had the most dangerous job. Even hobbled, some of the yearlings could get off a kick. Once the testicles were free, the number two threw the bloody nubs to the ranch dogs, which would fight over the prize. The smart dogs learned quickly and expended little energy on the squabble. Instead they bypassed the fracas to make sure they received the next pair. The number three man carried a bucket of axle grease and dabbed it onto the colt's empty sack. It was an assembly-line operation.

George Marlow was in charge today. He worked for Sun Boy, or "Pai-Taly" in Kiowa. Every August, Sun Boy weaned and castrated his horse colts for eventual sale to the army. He did this when the colts were about one year old. This often caused debates among his hands. Some were of the opinion that the colts should be at least two when they were cut; others favored an initial proud cut followed by complete casting at two. Whatever mixed opinions there were on gelding, they all disapproved of waiting a year for weaning. Sun Boy would not have it any other way. He was convinced that waiting improved each animal's constitution. He also believed that a horse should not have too many bad days and wanted the worst moments, gelding and weaning, to happen at the same time. The animals would soon recover and be sold in another year to the army. Sun Boy did not agree with gelding and refused to have it done to his private stock. The army, however, would not purchase stallions, so the late-summer casting and weaning were routine on the ranch.

The August event had become quite the celebration and was only slightly smaller than Fourth of July. There were army buyers, white citizens from nearby Lawton, and representatives from several tribes of the various reservations. George Marlow enjoyed it and was sorry his four brothers and mother were unable to attend. He had worked for Sun Boy for several years and was grateful for the job as well as the chief's kindness.

After the casting, a lottery would be held for steers that Sun Boy donated to certain families from each reservation. The steers were in a holding pen and would be turned loose. The braves would set out after them, representative of the old buffalo hunts. Since they were not allowed to have firearms, at least not where the army officers could see, they used bows and lances. Most of these young bucks had never seen a wild buff, much less hunted one, and this was their closest chance. The whites from Lawton and the officers sat in bleachers the chief had constructed for the event and would cheer the braves on. It was good medicine, and Sun Boy was well thought of for it.

George cut the last gelding free of the hobble and stood back as he, or it, was released. He directed the men to finish the cleanup and prepare for the steer hunt. As the cowboys began tearing down the riggings, George knelt to look at the grass. He ran his fingers through it and scratched around the dirt. This grass was Indian grass. Hopefully, when the territory opened to more settlers next spring, some of this would be Marlow grass. The grass was poor, as was the soil, and it had never supported any animals but buffalo. The buffalo were all gone; maybe cattle would do as well—Marlow cattle on Marlow grass. He and his family still did not own anything other than a small remuda and a few cattle. George was imagining a large house with numerous out-buildings when he was interrupted.

"You like my grass, Jorge?" It was Sun Boy, kneeling down beside him. The chief liked to call his white employees by their Spanish names. George did not know if the chief could speak Spanish or not. He probably could. He was a smart man.

The chief was dressed for the celebration. He wore a U.S. Army general's frock coat and a loincloth with no leggings. His hair was in tails and wrapped with otter fur. George had never seen an otter in the territory, and it always amazed him how every Comanche or Kiowa buck he knew wore the otter braids. For all he knew they mail-ordered them from the Montgomery & Ward catalog. Sun Boy wore different fashion for different events. If it was an Indian-only gathering, he was dressed accordingly. When the gathering was white, Sun Boy was dressed as any businessman back east, even sporting spats on occasion. The army officers liked to see him wearing their uniform. Some even endorsed the rumor that Sun Boy had killed a general back in the wild days and had taken the frock from him. It reminded them of old times, and most did not want to know that it had been a gift from no less than General Sherman some years before when the regulations dictated new attire. Sherman was fond of Sun Boy and had presented him with it while visiting his ranch.

The chief was not like pen-Indians and was probably not a real chief. After a few years on the reservation, he mastered the whites' business means and set out on his own. And every Sunday he was an usher in the Methodist church in Lawton—the white congregation, not the Indian one. While his fellow braves sat complacent and indignant on the reserve, he decided to conquer the whites at their interests. And he did, daily. He lived in a large three-story mansion with tepees behind it. He even had a sweat lodge and would no doubt have a good sweat today with some of the chiefs from the reservations. He would graciously invite the army officers, who would just as politely regret.

"Why are you looking at my grass, Jorge?" the chief asked again.

"Just thinking about it, and about when my family will have their own grass."

"Soon. You are welcome to it. As long as you leave mine alone." The chief smiled to show he meant no harm. "If you had not followed your dream chaser so long, you might even own my grass."

The "dream chaser" was George's father—Doctor Wilburn Williamson Marlow. The chief had fondly named him that. The chief and his father were both dream chasers, but the chief had a better sense of business. Doctor Marlow had followed many dreams right up until he was buried outside Sherman, Texas, three years prior. Since then George had tried to assume his father's mantle, with little success. The only success had been putting a stop to the family's ceaseless migration across the Southwest. George had little to do with this; it had been his mother who planned on homesteading and waiting on the 1889 opening of the territory. George kept playing with the grass. Sun Boy spoke again.

"You know, the Texans want this grass too. They are already here. They do not possess any grass yet in the territory, just steal it. Their herds are already here and they have many armed men. This grass is free for them. My people can no longer fight them for it. All Texans, especially the cattle barons, think Indians do not need the grass. The only reason we Indians are here is your people thought this land was worthless before the cattle."

"Now, wait a minute, I am not a Texan. They are not my people," George snapped.

Sun Boy smiled and patted his back. "You people all look alike to me." George smiled back at his disarming employer, who added, "You have spent enough time dreaming, *jaan*. Now go see to it my people can enjoy their hunt today." George liked it when the chief called him *jaan*, meaning "son" in Kiowa. He smiled again, got up, dusted his backside off, and walked with the chief over to the pens.

There were several hundred whites in the stands next to the cattle pens. At least fifty or so bucks were mounted and waiting in a staging area behind the fence. The braves' families, old men, wives, and children, further back still. Inside the corral, one hundred beeves stirred around, unaware of their pending contribution to the festivities.

George and the chief climbed up some steps built next to the fence, leading to a small platform. The chief offered an invocation to the Great Mystery and Grandmother Spider and urged every brave to do his utmost and bring honor on their families. When the chief finished, all the braves whooped and called out to each other in at least a dozen Indian languages. George did not know how all the bucks understood the chief's Kiowa. When the yelling died down somewhat, George explained to the whites what was about to happen. All the cattle were to be loosed and chased out onto the prairie. The chief would then signal to the braves to begin the hunt. George admonished all to look after their children and warned the ladies that they might wish to look away, lest the sight of blood upset them. George finished and looked to the chief. Sun Boy nodded, and several mounted men inside with the beeves began yelling and firing into the air. The cattle stirred for a moment at the hollering and made no movement toward the open gate until the firing began. As soon as they passed the gate, the stampede was on. As the cattle ran past the fence line, Chief gave his signal for the bucks to begin. The braves broke forth with their cries again and took off.

The hunt did not last long. Most of the animals were lanced or shot with arrows within sight of the bleachers, which was just fine with the chief and the crowd. The bucks were indifferent. A photographer from Lawton had set up to try and get some shots, but seemed disappointed in how quickly it was over. As each steer was hit, the braves' family ran out onto the plain and began cutting up the beast. No white ladies fainted until the braves, sometimes with their sons, cut out the animal's sweetmeats and began eating them right out of the cavity.

George followed the chief to farewell his white guests. For his employees and most of the Indians, the festivities would continue into the night. But the white guests needed to understand that their welcome was at an end. The day's remainder was more familial and might be thought barbaric by the whites. Dancing, gaming, and sweats would last into the evening.

Sun Boy worked the crowd, as skillful as any politician, with George smiling and greeting by his side. George heard a commotion behind him on the plain. He continued smiling and stole a glance over his shoulder, back toward the gory field. Four bucks were arguing with a family in the process of cutting up a steer. The family consisted of a young woman with two boys and an old man. The father was probably dead or drunk on the reservation, and the old man, a grandfather. He was fussing but was ignored by the younger, stronger bucks. Suddenly, one of the bucks pushed him down to the ground. The woman tried to attack the brave with her skinning knife, but she was quickly grabbed by one of his confederates, disarmed, and pushed down alongside the grandfather. One of the little boys began to cry. George normally would have alerted the chief but did not want to interrupt. He decided to manage it himself. Walking the hundred yards out into the fields, he whistled at the family, who had already accepted the piracy and were leaving. George motioned them back. He would right this. The family stopped but did not move back to the carrion, only watched.

George walked up smiling, an attempt to be peaceable. The thieves were finishing the sweetmeats started by the family. Already their hands and mouths were covered in yellow gall and blood from the feast. He asked the buck who had pushed the old man what the story was. The brave did not answer or even look at George. George asked again. Again, the braves ignored him. George pulled his gun. He understood little Indian but said, "*Miar*," "go" in Comanche. He hoped at least one of them understood. The big one looked up, took one last bite of liver, nudged his comrades, and walked away. George watched them for a bit, then motioned for the family to return. The old man said nothing, turned, and walked back toward the reservation.

"What in the Sam Hill..." George said aloud, holstering his gun.

"You embarrassed the old man, Jorge." It was Sun Boy, standing behind him. George wondered how much he had seen, or if he would be upset.

"I was just trying to help him." George replied.

"I know. Your ways are not ours. If he had wanted your help, he would have asked. You need to be wary of those four bucks for a while. They will remember you." Sun Boy changed the subject, as he was known to do whenever the conversation got too grim. "Come, help me get the rest of your people off my land before they try to steal any more of it." Sun Boy put his arm around George and smiled as they walked back toward the stands.

"It is all right here. I do not believe you care much for the business of this county or the citizens who pay your salary," Frank Harmonson shouted.

Young County Sheriff Marion DeKalb Wallace sat behind his desk staring at nothing, which seemed to be on the opposite side of the wall he was facing. Right in the middle of Frank Harmonson's protests and expletives concerning stock rustlers, the sheriff had gone wall-eyed, no expression whatsoever. It was as if Harmonson and County Attorney P. A. Martin were not even present. Not that Wallace paid much attention to them even when he didn't go gooch-faced. Of course, he couldn't totally ignore Martin, whom he received his caseload from. The stock in question was being absconded in Indian Territory, and Wallace, being a county official, had no jurisdiction there. Most of the stock belonged to local ranchers who ran their herd north of Red River, and they were up in arms about the situation. Even though Graham was the federal court for the territory, it just was not county business.

In Harmonson's mind, Wallace wasn't working with Federal Deputy Marshal Ed Johnson enough to stem the tide of thievery. Eleven years before, the Texas Cattle Raisers Association had formed in Graham and had become quite the political force, with the means to back it up. That was Harmonson's big casino. He was, or at least he believed he was, the association's mouthpiece and seemed to be doing a fine job of it too, until the sheriff went to woolgathering right in the middle of what appeared to be a well-rehearsed soliloquy.

Young County Deputy Tom Collier sat opposite Wallace with his chair leaned back against the wall and his feet propped up on the sheriff's desk. He was bored, though amused, and had pulled out his Barlow to work on his fingernails. If they hadn't company, he would've mined on his toes a bit as well. Wallace barely trusted Collier and knew it would not be long before the backstabber began passing this information around the saloons and amongst the townies. If not to Marshal Johnson or the barons themselves.

The jail they were in was fairly modern, as modern went. The entrance faced north and fronted Fourth Street about one block east off the town square. It was two-storied, of sandstone construction, with nice oak floors and ceilings. The first floor was the front office and was strictly for public transactions, such as the one currently going on. In the rear were the kitchen and living quarters of the turnkey, Joe Leavell. Even though nearly thirty years old, he was still unmarried and thought immature. He wasn't much of a jailer either. Half the time he left the cells wide open because he couldn't find the one key that his entire job title was based upon. He was a pig too. Joe liked his comfort, so in the winter, though mild in West Texas, he used an old chamber pot he found from somewhere that he kept under his bunk, and not wanting to stray from his warm environs or let his feet hit the cold floor, he would just lean out of bed a ways and make water or take a movement right there. He didn't even clean the bowl out, just dumped the contents in the old sink out back every so often.

No one knew for how long that went on, but eventually the stench began to overwhelm some of the prisoners on the second floor right above Leavell's bed. The odd part about it was that the jail had an indoor water closet, one of the first in Graham. People still stopped by now and again to admire the in-house porcelain, and some even stopped long enough to take an indulgence, but not Joe. Wallace was so angry he made him live out of one of the cells upstairs for a week to teach him a lesson and let the room air out.

On the second floor were the two jail cells that housed the odd drunk or cowpuncher who got out of line. The building was reasonably warm during the winter—except for Leavell's room apparently—but during the summer months became a furnace and sometimes caused prisoners upstairs to faint. The window bars on the cells were hot to the touch. So in the heat of the day, county business often as not would be conducted outside on the porch, where the constant plains breeze cooled folks off a bit.

Today was a little overcast, which made the air more tolerable, so Wallace had decided to conduct business indoors. Besides, clouds brought rain, and Wallace was not a man to get wet if he could prevent it. One time, chasing some waddies that had shot up one of the establishments, Wallace and Collier were caught up in a thunder-squall. The drovers went to ground in a cave on Elm Creek and seemed determined not to go with the two county representatives. They were snuggled up and dry while the duly appointed sat in their fish; two wet, miserable lawmen on two wet, miserable horses. Wallace soon forgot about the felonious behavior of the arid desperados and convinced them that all charges would be dropped if their 'fraid hole might be shared. Later, when Collier questioned the sheriff, all Wallace offered was some fragment of an oath he had sworn to himself during the war not to ever be wet again.

The men had come back from the war seasoned, but Wallace was one of those who returned like he had left a portion of himself back on some battlefield. He didn't carry a grudge about it like some veterans around Graham did, and was not one to bring the matter up much, but every once in a while he would just fade. This mostly happened when he was drinking, which he did often and to excess.

"Damn it, Sheriff, are you listening to me?"

Just then Wallace sat bolt upright and stared at the three men, especially Harmonson. His vacant stare turned to curiosity the harder he looked at Harmonson. Wallace considered him the biggest bastard in town. He felt that he was back in the present. He did not revisit the war during daylight. It normally was at night that all his old pards came to see him. He shook his head and he looked at Harmonson, all the way up and down again. Then he spoke.

"Where in the Sam Hill did you get that outfit, Columbus?" It was a good question, Collier had to admit, and he had considered asking it himself but had let it pass, figuring the subject would eventually come up. Harmonson was wearing a normal sack suit; it was, however, bright red with black squares. It was a flasharity, not that fancy was bad fashion in Graham. The trail drivers who would pass through always dressed gaily, and the Indians camped on Salt Creek could hold their own as well. But this suit was a sight. Harmonson's frustration at the situation turned to anger, not only because of the outfit comment, but because Wallace had called him by his true first name, "Columbus," which he detested. It was kind of a gift that Wallace had, to be able to put men off their direction with a comment like that. It worked this time just as it always had.

"By God, you drunk, you will not talk to me like that—I can buy you over and again."

"While you are at it, why don't you buy some new duds as well? People 'round here might go blind with you running around like that. I am apt to charge you with public endangerment," Wallace calmly fired back.

Harmonson's forehead and ears turned a color that seemed to match his suit—not with shame but with rage. Little balls of sweat formed on his brow and he started to speak, but the sheriff cut him off again.

"I mean, Columbus, you look like a tablecloth. I am going to have to ask you to leave. Otherwise the prisoners will think it is time for sup, and we don't have any grub for them yet. You could be the cause of a riot, so git. P. A., you can stay and visit, but the suit has got to go." Collier thought it odd that the sheriff mentioned prisoners, since there weren't any in jail at present, but he thought better of correcting him just now. Wallace leaned over and began plowing through his desk drawers as if the matter was solved, and his guests departed.

"Fine, you sonofabitch, fine. We will see where this ends up." Harmonson pulled on his Stetson so hard that Collier thought he would pull the brim away from the crown. He glared at P. A., who was enjoying this far too much.

"Come on, 'Phlete,' let us go see if Deputy United States Marshal Ed Johnson can assist the property owners of this county." Not wanting to be caught short on poor choices for first names, he had called the county attorney by his given name as well. Wallace just sat there looking back and forth between the two of them, forcing a puzzled look on his face to feign innocence in the matter. Harmonson stamped out of the office and down the hall, which was festooned with wanted posters and other legal bric-a-brac that nobody ever read. Harmonson set such a pace that he caused a breeze to stir, and the papers tacked to the wall rustled as he passed. Martin stopped at the office door, turned and looked back at the pair, shrugged his shoulders, and followed.

Harmonson attempted to slam the front door on his exit, but the turnkey had latigo'd the knob back to a nail in the wall so the door could remain open and permit a breeze when the wind was just right. Harmonson put his hand on the frame and attempted to slam the last word of the discussion, but the leather was stronger and the door only budged slightly forward and then jerked back against the taut hide. All they heard inside was a barely audible expletive and his stampeding footsteps, with Martin in tow down the walk heading toward the square and, no doubt, the marshal's office.

United States Deputy Marshal Edward W. Johnson's office was just south and west across the square from the Young County jail. The square was large even by Texas standards. On the north side, saloons were the principal business, while various other emporiums divided the remainder. Voters had chosen Graham as the county seat some years before, but it was still a sensitive topic among folks in the other municipals, especially since Graham was the newest incorporated. Two Kentucky brothers named E. S. and E. A. Graham had started a saltworks down off a fork of the Brazos River. The work prospered, the brothers did well, and as a consequence Graham flourished, and the seat moved to the town a few years back. The town did well supporting the ranchers, buffalo hunters, and various merchants who soon moved in. The Indians had either died off or been moved out by the army, which moved out as well following the red man's demise. As a result of Graham's bounty, her citizens had built the square as a living monument to that fruitfulness, with a large county courthouse as its centerpiece. Eventually, it was hoped, the railhead a mile north of the square would be a major stop for the state. The town even had a few telephones. They weren't operational in many places, but they soon would be.

And that was what Frank Harmonson was about: progress, industry, and business. Right now it might mean the cattle barons were calling all the shots, but circumstances were bound to change, and he wouldn't have to lap-dog the ranchers anymore. The balance of power would shift and he would be the he-bull.

Harmonson didn't speak a word crossing Elm Street on the way to the federal court building. All he could think about was getting the sheriff out of office as soon as possible. Problem was Wallace's overwhelming popularity and undeniable political skills. He was good on the stump and in the saloons; people liked him and overlooked his drinking. Most of them drank to excess as well; why shouldn't the sheriff? But he was so shortsighted that he never could see what Young County could become. Marshal Johnson, conversely, was a federally appointed imbecile whose only purpose in life was constantly bemoaning that he hadn't been old enough to fight in the war. Even had daguerreotypes taken of himself wearing his father's Confederate uniform. Whereas Wallace had maybe seen too much, Johnson hadn't seen any, not in the war anyway, and as a consequence was constantly trying to prove himself more of a man than his counterpart across the square.

Only a few years before, during some shady business dealing with Frank James of Missouri fame in Wichita Falls, Johnson had lost his right arm in a gunfight. Nobody knew too much about it, and Johnson wasn't talking. From the gossip, it seemed he had mouthed off about the James' infamous Minnesota raid one too many times, so Frank had calmly pulled his heater and blown off Johnson's right arm for the trouble. He didn't blow it off entirely, and for a while it just hung there with the marshal hoping it would heal back some. A lawman in Texas without his gun arm was a liability both to himself and his duties. The arm didn't seem to be healing, so Johnson worked a deal with one of the Kiowa medicine men who had camped down on the Salt Fork of the Brazos. Since Graham was the federal court for the Indian Territory, there was always a variety of tribes down on the fork waiting for their time with the judge. The healer, whether out of meanness toward the "white-eye" or just by accident, worked up quite a cure for the marshal, and pretty soon the bad arm started looking worse, smelling, and it swelled up till it split his shirtsleeves. Joe Leavell had found Johnson passed out in his own vomit and talking about Jeff Davis. The doctor sawed the arm off while he was in his delirium. When Johnson recovered, he tried to find the Kiowa but couldn't, and Sheriff Wallace threatened to shoot off the other arm if he bothered the sawbones.

The square was busy. Not too much, but enough that Martin began to get concerned over Harmonson's gait as he stormed across the Young County Courthouse lawn, then to the edge of Oak Street. As soon as they hit the second street of the square, Martin had to grab his companion's sleeve to keep him from stepping out in front of a remuda that some local cowboys were moving toward the train station just north of town. At first he looked back at Martin like he was deranged but saw the danger and gave him an obliging nod. They clipped by at a good pace, stirring up more than the usual amount of road dust and turning Harmonson's suit from gunfire red to a dirty pink. As soon as Harmonson noticed the dust on his new suit, he went off again.

Harmonson gestured toward the passing horses. "There, you see, P. A., that is what I am talking about. Wallace will not even look to the citizens' safety. People riding at any speed through here. Hood did not leave Atlanta as fast as those rascals were moving." Martin nodded as much and motioned for Frank that the street was now clear. They continued across the street with Harmonson swearing and dusting off his suit.

The two men entered the large federal building on Oak Street. It was new and it was nice. The floors were highly buffed at the insistence of Judge A. P. McCormick, late of Dallas, now of Graham. The folks in Young County had wanted to be highbrow, and they reasoned that a U.S. federal judge living amongst them might class life up a bit. To get him to move to Graham from Dallas had been quite a job, and the city fathers built him a house befitting his station. It worked. The judge moved in, but it remained to be decided whether the living conditions in Graham had improved or not.

The building stood vacant except for an old Indian in a blanket wrap warming a bench outside of the main courtroom. He looked straight at the men as they passed to the stairs beside him and even craned his neck around to see them as they took their first few steps. Harmonson hadn't noticed him on the way in but always had the gift of sensing someone staring at him. After the first couple of steps, he stopped so suddenly that Martin nearly ran into him. Frank turned around and stared at the Indian, who was staring up at him. Martin saw Harmonson's face get that look in it again, but he remained silent as his companion kept glaring at the Indian. Martin thought it must have been a minute that had passed, when finally Frank boiled over and screamed, "WHAAAAT?" at the top of his lungs. The red man didn't flinch. Just said, "Nice suit." Then the Indian turned back around to continue his business at hand, whatever that was. Harmonson shook violently for a moment, and then his rage passed. He coughed, wet his lips, straightened his coat, and headed back up the stairs to the marshal's office.

CHAPTER 2

COMANCHE INDIAN RESERVATION
FORT SILL, INDIAN TERRITORY

The first impression about Fort Sill was the enormous number of Indians present, especially when compared to soldiers. A European passing through might mistake it for an Indian fort where the bluecoats were prisoners. That was not the case, though, and Sill was the final home for the nomads who once controlled the Great Plains from the lower Rockies to the Río Grande.

Most of the Indians seemed resigned to their new life as wards of the state, and some of them even flourished. Kiowa Chief Sun Boy kept a lively and thriving camp that included everything from mercantile to livestock and employed mostly whites. George Marlow wondered why other Indians did not fare as well as the chief. George was in Sill to close out some accounts for the chief and was working his way down the street to settle the business.

The ride from Sun Boy's camp had taken all morning, and George could feel it in his legs and the balls of his feet. He stopped in front of an emporium, dismounted slowly, and tethered his horse, "Shoat." There was never any end to the grief caused by a horse named after a pig once folks found out. Other than providing entertainment, often at George's expense, the horse was fine. Sometimes when the family had dinner together, the subject would come up until their mother put an end to it.

The gelding was a fine mount, and George had taken him up and down the trail several times and had no reason to regret the animal.

He tied off the reins and loosed the girth. Then he stretched and squatted to force some of the blood around his rump, which had gone to sleep altogether. Shoat was foamed, even though George had walked him for the last five miles. He figured about twenty minutes in the store, barring any problems, and then he could grain and water the horse. While he was bent down on his haunches and finishing his stretch, a pair of brogans with beaded leggings appeared in front of his face. At first he thought he might be in someone's way, so he pardoned himself and moved a little. The leggings didn't. George moved slowly, realizing his poor position if this were to be a fight. He lifted his head, following the body until he made eye contact. It was noon and the sun was in his view. But he could tell that the leggings were attached to an Indian, a big one. The same buck George had chased off the reservation last week. And he had his friends with him.

"Hidy." George smiled. It was forced, but he did not need a fight just now, sprawled on the ground with three or four bucks standing over him.

"You steal Indian's pony."

Still smiling, George lifted himself from the ground and began dusting off his seat and took a few steps back so he could not be rushed. He was guilty of a few sins in his life—stealing was not one of them. George knew this was not about Shoat; it was about the beeve. The smile faded. "Indian lies. I bought this pony and it is mine."

The brave grunted, moved to the front of the horse, and began untying him from the post. As soon as he touched the reins, George Marlow moved quickly around the horse's croup, jerked and cocked his sidearm, and placed it under the Indian's nose. To the buck's credit, George reflected later, he did not flinch—just looked back and met his glare.

"Now, look here, I have never had cause to hurt one of you people, but I will if I am pushed too far. So drop that rein and disappear at once, or you will find yourself in the happy hunting grounds." The brave said nothing, didn't even look at the pistol, only at George.

One of the Indians seemed to be more of a peacemaker and spoke quietly to his horse-poor companion. The words were in Comanche, but George knew that he was trying to mollify his partner. The pistol was not going to move until the reins were dropped. The buck nodded and took his hand away from the post.

"Indian Agent," the buck said.

"What about him? This is none of his concern." George decided not to drop the gun just yet. A small crowd was beginning to form. None were taking sides, but George believed they might soon. One man from the crowd, who apparently understood the language, spoke. "They want you to go to the commanding officer, and you had better go, as that is the best way to settle the matter." This was not his territory, so George holstered and motioned for the buck to lead the way.

The agent's office was only one building up, so George decided the horse would be fine. Just the same, he stood by the door and made sure all involved went into the building ahead of him. Indian Agent Edward E. White's office was small and worn. There were two desks, and only one of those appeared utilized; the other was stacked with numerous piles of paper varying from about six to twelve inches high. Supplies were scattered around in either barrels or sacks, and in the corner was a large scale that had a "Do not use for beef" sign hanging from it.

The building appeared empty until there was a noise from the rear through the back door, which was marked with lettering that spelled out "Warehouse." There seemed to be a concern occurring on the other side of it, and George could just make out muffled directives and profanities and the sound of people and crates moving about. The braves walked around George and went over to the desk that employed all the stacks and squatted on the floor, as was their custom, and waited. Several minutes passed while the bucks sat on haunches motionless, with George fidgeting, as was his custom, standing near the front door so he could watch both the Indians and Shoat.

The warehouse door opened and what appeared to be a clerk, complete with sleeve-stockings and apron, stepped through with his arms full of documents. He moved gingerly over to the busy desk, oblivious to everyone in the office. He set the papers on the desk, taking several seconds, apparently deciding which pile they belonged in. Once the papers were according, he looked up and noticed the braves and George Marlow in his environs.

"Howdy, boys," he said to the Indians and to George, rather shortly. "I'm Kiowa Agent White, what do you need?"

Before George could even introduce himself, the Indians started in with their native tongue and all together. He thought it sounded like they were speaking different languages, but he wasn't sure. Agent White just stood there with his arms folded, nodding and occasionally asking a question of them. After several minutes of the guttural vernacular, White appeared satisfied with the Indians' side of the story. He looked at George.

"How long have you owned the horse?"

"My name is George Marlow and I purchased the hoss from Ed Walsh. I can produce a bill of sale if given the time. These Comanche are accusing me of stealing my own pony."

"Calm yourself, Mr. Marlow. You know better than to travel without a receipt. And besides, there is only one Comanche in here and that is Black Crow, who claims that 'your' horse is 'his' pony. The other is Bar-Sinda-Bar, who is Caddo. I do not know the other two, but they are Kiowa. You have sure stirred up the pot to have this many nations represented against you. I will call the question again; how long have you owned the horse?" the agent repeated, slightly annoyed at the redundancy.

"About six months," George replied. The braves retained their position on the floor, turning their heads to whomever was talking. Agent White told this to the Indians and produced what looked like a receipt from one of his piles and appeared to be asking Black Crow if he had one. Black Crow muttered something and stared at George. White nodded and put back the paper onto the menagerie before him. He walked around the desk, at the same time excusing himself, in whatever language, from the aborigines. Crossing the room, he stood inches away from George's face and spoke very softly.

"I do not have no crystal ball, mister. The only thing for sure is one of you is lying. My reputation would be worth little with the white folks of this hole if I took the bucks' side. Skedaddle."

George could smell dill pickle on Agent White's breath and maybe some mint as well. "Skedaddle? What service are you going to provide me to keep them from taking my hoss as soon as we walk out of here?"

"Well, if you let these Indians take your horse, it is your fault." George needed no further motivation and deduced that there would be no friendly intervention on the side of the agent. He mumbled a begrudged 'Thankee' and was out the door.

His daddy had told him that men on foot never run in the rain or when they're in trouble, so George slowed his pace down to a quick step, listening for the agent's door to open or footsteps thundering up from behind. He walked up to Shoat, untied him from the post, and put his foot to the stirrup. There were no other horses parked at the hitch, so he would be able to make a quick turnaround and get out of Sill. As soon as his weight went up on his leg, the saddle shifted... the cinch was still loosed. Just then the door to the agent's office slammed open and the four braves exploded onto the porch. His pa had never said anything about a man on horseback running. George pulled himself up by Shoat's mane and quickly swung his right leg over the horse and found his other stirrup. The girth would have to wait.

George spun Shoat around, raking with both spurs, and opened him up back toward home. Unfortunately the direction of home meant passing the Indians, who were none too happy just now. He considered his gun again but thought better of it. He was never as good a shot as his brother Boone and might miss and hit an innocent. Even if his aim was true, he did not want to face a federal court for killing an Indian on Fort Sill.

The braves bolted for George, attempting to cut him off as he passed the agent's office. They were yelling to each other and whooping the way they were known to. Apparently the Indians were not adept at foot sports, because they never came close to George and Shoat. As George neared the end of the street, he stole a glance back and noticed they were gone. He kept up his gait toward the house.

Some miles out of Sill, George slowed up his pace a bit. Every so often he kept looking over his shoulder, but there was no sign of the bucks. Shoat was well lathered and it was still the heat of the day. George couldn't remember when he had watered him last, but it had been a while. He stopped to step out of the saddle and give Shoat some refreshment from his own water bottle. As soon as his weight shifted, so did the saddle, which still had a loose cinch. George landed flat on his back, and the wind in him almost escaped from both ends at the same time. He lay there and looked up at the horse.

"Not only are you named for a pig, you manage to look like a wild Indian's hoss too. I could be dead right now and they would be riding you to hunt their agency beeves, pretending like they was buffalo." He got up and began fixing the saddle and his trail gear, which had come askew during the fracas. Once the tack was secure, he took off his Stetson and filled it with water. Shoat could smell the liquid as soon as George opened the canteen, and the horse let out an approving noise and stomped his feet. George stuck the crown under the horse's nose and let him drink. George figured that two hatfuls should keep him until they got back to the house. He had decided to head for his family's place rather than his employer's. Home was closer, so it had seemed natural at the time. It was almost like he was a kid—get in trouble and run for home. George was not expected back at the chief's camp from Sill until tomorrow, and Sun Boy would understand.

Shoat lifted his muzzle from the hat and looked back toward the fort. His ears were erect and he blew his nostrils. George immediately cursed himself for a fool. He had stopped in a small depression and had no clear view behind him. He put his hand over the animal's nose, shushed him, and listened. There was only quiet, not even a breeze. He shouldn't have stopped; they were only a few miles from the family cabin. George quietly and quickly tied the canteen behind the cantle, pulled his hat back on, and stepped into the saddle. When his right foot hit the stirrup, he felt it jerk inward and heard a *thunk*. The inward jerk on the stirrup caused Shoat to bolt, and George was almost pitched from the saddle. When he looked down to his stirrup he noticed an arrow imbedded in it and then saw the mounted Indian who shot it crossing the crest and pulling for a second try.

George gave Shoat the reins and dug in both spurs. The forward movement caused the brave to miss his aim, and the bolt passed behind him. The four bucks were well within pistol shot and had not calmed their passions any at all. Once away from the gully and back onto the plain, George drew for the second time that day, which was more than he had done all year, then half turned in the saddle and fired a shot back into his pursuers. The Indians were completely naked except for breechcloths and had covered themselves and their mounts in war paint. George thought he even saw scalps hanging from one of their quivers, but he wasn't sure and was not planning on getting close enough to find out.

The brief respite had done Shoat well, and he was leaving ground and moving out of bow range. George did not believe there were any firearms on the Indians, as they were not allowed to carry them. Just then he heard a *zing* past his ear, followed by the report of a rifle. It appeared that Agent White had not been doing his job. George was not going to think on that right now, only on home.

The braves kept up their pursuit. Now and again one or two of them would drop out of sight for a while and then reappear moments later. George had understood that braves could make water while on horseback; maybe that was a myth and they were taking turns relieving themselves. It felt like this had been on for hours. George had only fired one shot, in order to conserve ammo. He knew it was useless, as poor a shot as he was, to fire from a horse. Shoat was foamed and frothy from his mouth all the way to his croup and was beginning to stumble a little from exhaustion. The animal was not going to last much longer. George did not know how the braves kept up their gait, and with horses that had run after him all the way from Sill. Sun Boy had told him that the Indian pony was magical and would always be stronger and faster than a horse ridden by a white man. George thought, *If Shoat goes down, maybe they will leave and not want him.* He was a good horse, but there was little magic to him, especially now.

George was lost in thought and fear as he came up a slight rise in the prairie. The ground suddenly became familiar to him and the horse. Just about one mile away was the Marlow dugout and Wild Horse Creek. Home. He could even see his brothers working around the barn. He immediately pulled his sidearm and began firing it wildly over his head. He knew that as soon as his family heard the shots they would come fast.

The clan had been busy, but as the noise of the firing hit the homestead, they all looked up at once from their chores at hand. Charley was the first to speak.

"Is that George? He sure is riding fast."

"Why is he shootin'?" asked Lewellyn. He hated the name and insisted on being called "Elly" or "Epp." The question answered itself. Just behind George, his four brothers noticed an equal number of Indians closing fast behind him. They were shooting too.

The Marlow family moved. It almost seemed rehearsed; three brothers went after the horses, while Boone, the youngest, ran inside to get the hardware. It was a good thing their mother was at church, else she would slow everyone down, and George needed them now. By the time Boone had grabbed their weapons, or at least all he could find, the three brothers and four horses were outside and saddled. Charley was yelling at Boone, "Come on!" He lit out the door with his arms full of guns and ammo boxes, stopping by every sibling to issue his. As soon as each brother received, they took off toward George in turn. Normally they waited for one another, but this situation was not normal.

George had noticed the brothers sprint for the house and barn but had passed into another depression and lost sight of them. When he came back out, he saw no one. He was so close. The horse tripped again for the last time and went down on his knees and chest. The sudden stopping of Shoat had caused George to propel over the top of his head at the same speed they had been moving prior to the stumble. He tried to recover, but it was too late. The ejection had caused him to drop his firearm and knocked him dizzy as well. He forgot all about the Indians and his brothers. All he could remember was that he needed his gun back in his hand.

The four Marlow brothers caught up with each other and were riding straight down on George, but they wouldn't arrive before the Indians did. Shoat had stumbled or been shot and George was on all fours crawling on the ground. He was in a bad way. He did not notice his three brothers passing or recognize Boone's voice as he dismounted and knelt down beside him.

"George, are ya shot?"

"No. Just shot at," George whispered almost. He kept crawling and looking for his dropped revolver. Boone reached down and pulled his brother's face up to his, "George, it is me, your brother Boone. We have chased the Indians away. Alf, Charley, and Elly are still after them. I am to take you back to the cabin."

George finally recognized his brother but was still dim on the situation. Boone walked over and got Shoat, who was winded and a little skinned up, but still rideable. He helped George up on him, threw his catch rope around the horse's head, and led them both back to the dugout.

Darkness always came late in the summer. It was at about the twilight when George and Boone noticed the horses gathering outside. They heard their brothers talking and laughing, then it faded as they moved to the corral to let the horses cool down before their fodder. A few minutes later, Charley walked in. He was filthy.

"You look like you just come off the cow trail," Boone said.

"I feel like it too. How is George?"

"I am fine. What happened?" George was seated at what passed for the table.

"I might ask you the same question." Charley dusted himself off a bit and went in to sit on the bench by the hearth.

"I did not know we was still fighting red Indians. We chased them another few miles before their hosses gave. Once they were afoot, the fight sort of just left 'em. We took the stock and the weapons and sent them back to Fort Sill walking. What were they after you for anyways?"

George waited until all his brothers were inside. He thanked them and recounted his story.

It was well past dark when the braves, on foot, arrived back at Sill. They were ashamed and kept fussing at Black Crow for causing them to lose their horses and honor. They would be little better than women once they got back and could afford no more horses.

Black Crow remained quiet. He acknowledged to himself the grief he had caused and was going to make it right. Stealing more horses was no good and they would be caught. He decided to use the white man's law for his own. He would tell the agent that a white gang of brothers had followed them and stolen their remuda and they would have no way to provide for their families this fall. The others followed him to the agent's office and watched as he sat down on the sidewalk out front and waited for Agent White to open the door in the morning.

CHAPTER 3

TELEGRAPHER'S OFFICE
GRAHAM, TEXAS

*J*oe Bishop reread the telegram he had just received:

DEPUTY MARSHAL EDWARD W. JOHNSON:
LOOK OUT FOR THE FIVE MARLOW BROTHERS WHO ARE
ENDEAVORING TO GET AWAY WITH FORTY HEAD OF HORSES
STOLEN FROM THIS PLACE.
AGENT EDWARD E. WHITE
KIOWA AGENCY, FORT SILL, INDIAN TERRITORY

Bishop knew that the message must get to Marshal Johnson's office at once. The confusing jurisdiction of the Indian Territory was always problematic. It was divided, not equally, between Arkansas, Texas, and Colorado. The federal court in Graham had the largest jurisdiction, including the agencies around Fort Sill. By "this place" Agent White must have meant Fort Sill. Why else would he send it to Graham?

For over a decade, Bishop had been the single telegrapher for Young County and was respected for his duties by the townspeople. He had learned his trade in the Confederate Signal Service during the war. His primary specialty had been semaphore, but there was no real need for that outside of the army.

People hated to see him, though, as he rarely brought welcome news with his presence. On the streets, folks would glance up from their particulars, see him, and change direction. It would have bothered a lesser man, yet Bishop took pride in his appointment, perverse though it might have been from time to time.

He looked around his office for the boy he had hired to deliver the business-related messages. He saved himself for the formal ones. The child was nowhere around. Bishop, hoping no other transmission came in, stuffed the paper into an envelope, making sure the addressee's name showed through the cutout window on the front. He had just received these envelopes from the Western Union Company and was proud of them.

He stood up and took off his spectacles and put on his sack coat. It disturbed him to see the younger men in town in shirtsleeves. The war had brought an informality to the South that made Bishop uncomfortable. Shirtsleeves were fine for labor in a field or as a mechanic, or even inside with your own family. But outside for all to see, well, that was beyond the pale. Joe Bishop checked his thoughts. Often he would have out-loud conversations with himself or at least wave his arms around or slap down his hand to make a point inside his head. He tried to be careful about that.

The thought occurred to him, as it did now and again, that he should have a telephone fixed in here. He did not see the end of the telegram just yet, but the recent invention was all the commotion. More and more people greeted each other with that annoying "Hello," as opposed to just plain nodding or a "Howdy." The telephone might be here to stay, but Joe hoped that hello would pass quickly from fashion.

The telegraph office was located on Fourth Street across from the Young County Jail. Once outside his office, he pulled his keys to lock the door, remembered the boy, and thought better of it. He would have to leave official company property unsecure... again. Stupid child. Bishop was aware that the boy was probably out trying to get a glimpse into one of the jenny-barns on the north side of the square. From time to time, some group of ladies or one of the churches tried to get them thrown out of the county or at least out of town limits. It never seemed to work, and the whorehouses always rode out the brimstone and seemed to do a lot of business regardless.

The walk to Marshal Johnson's office took little time, as he was rushed. The downstairs of the federal building was empty, and Bishop walked straight up the stairs to the marshal's office. He didn't bother knocking on the door. It was already open a little, and Bishop had a mission and no time for formalities. Marshal Johnson was in his chair, his back to the door and his feet stretched straight out before him. He appeared to be on tiptoe, with his boots pointed at the wall facing him.

The toes of the boots gingerly touched the paneling. He had his good arm and nub stretched out beside him and his head was tilted back somewhat. On his nose was a butcher knife that was precariously balanced. He seemed all absorbed in it and kept doing his dance with his feet and his arm to maintain the knife's horizontal.

Joe Bishop had heard the stories about the man's eccentricities but considered it none of his concern. He watched for what must have been a full minute. He was afraid to speak for fear of the knife falling into the marshal's lap and amputating another extremity. The marshal started turning himself in his swivel chair by moving his toes along the wall. That seemed to Bishop the point of it. To turn all the way around and not drop the knife. Perhaps it was something those in the law practiced to improve the dexterity. Bishop wasn't sure.

Johnson kept his circuitous gyration going until he was back around and facing his desk. Once around, he gave himself a rather proud look, reached up, and removed the blade. He noticed Joe Bishop, realized he had probably seen his movements, and blushed. Bishop was used to people feeling awkward in his presence and had already let it pass.

"Marshal, we just received a telegram for you from an Agent White at the Kiowa Reservation near Fort Sill." He handed the envelope to Johnson and was distressed when the marshal didn't even glance at or seem to appreciate the envelope's window or the way Bishop had folded it just right so that only Johnson's name read through the cutout. The marshal placed the document on his desk and scratched at his missing limb while he read it. During the war, Bishop had heard that most amputations were done poorly and folks could always feel an itch or a pain in a limb that was long since gone.

Johnson finished reading and scratching, stuffed the paper into his pocket, and made for the door. "Thank you, Mr. Bishop." And was out of the office. Joe Bishop followed him at a distance out of the building. Once out in the air, he noticed the marshal walking toward one of the saloons, and Joe considered walking around the back to see if he could catch his boy helper on a landing, peeking into one of the brothels. Not wanting to be away from his duties, however, he went back to his office to wait for more messages on the wires.

There was that one back room in Jeffery's Saloon at Fourth and Oak streets, where all the swells held court. They had been idle all summer and would soon be gone for the fall roundups. Summer was the only time that they could all be found, and in one place. The barons had been on his backside for months concerning the rustler problems north of the Red. Marshal Johnson had always gotten to the territories fresh on a cold trail, and the stock kept being stolen. Never had names or descriptions of any miscreants. Sometimes they rode shod ponies and the next time they would be unshod. Johnson had hired Indian trackers from the reservations, but even that didn't work. Now he had names, now he had something to show the barons. It mattered little to Johnson if these were the same rustlers or whether they were guilty or not.

Ed Johnson walked into the saloon. The green, felt-covered gaming tables were mostly closed and wouldn't open for another few hours; then this place would be lit up good. The barons in their back room would all be gone home to their families and acting proper by that time. They owned all the bars and brothels, and most of the other businesses too, and paid their cowboys in Yankee dollars, which in turn were spent on their whiskey and whores. It all ended up back in the barons' wallets. Bartenders, whores, and the barons didn't have much concern outside of their wallets. And on church meeting, they would be in their front pew, with the family name inscribed upon a fancy brass plaque that the deacons had ordered from the Montgomery & Ward catalog. They had it all wrapped pretty tight—except for the herds on open rangeland north of the river.

Johnson caught the eye of the bartender. The keep stopped mopping the bar and nodded back over his shoulder toward the room.

"Marshal, I know you are not walking through my bar with your spurs on."

"It ain't *your* bar. I believe it belongs to them," Johnson replied, pointing toward the room.

"Maybe so, but they pay me to operate it, and you need to take off your hooks or leave." A couple of the local drunks with big mouths and stomachs for gossip were giggling like schoolgirls and poking each other in the ribs. The two had been dry all day, and the card games were all sour. Seeing the marshal put in his place picked their morale right up. Johnson, embarrassed, grabbed a chair from a nearby table and unbuttoned his spur straps. To get the last word in, he flung them onto the bar, where he hoped they scratched it.

"There was no need to do that." The keep grabbed the spurs almost as soon as they hit the top and flung them behind the bar.

"There was no need to talk to me like you did either." The drunks enjoyed this and were hooting and slapping, and Johnson saved some face. He turned around, enjoying the moment, and walked to the rear of the building and the room.

He stopped for a moment outside of the door to gather his thoughts. As usual, there were no sounds emanating from the room, so it was impossible to detect the mood. The news he brought seemed welcome, but the barons and their lackey Harmonson always added their particular turn. He knocked. From inside came the sound of movement and the doorknob turning. A tiny fade of light appeared through the jamb, followed by an overwhelming stench of cigars. An eye, belonging to Harmonson, peeked at him beyond the crack in the door.

"Come in, Marshal." The door pulled back, revealing the room. It was windowless, and only a single lamp burned on the table. There was a sense of coolness that confused Johnson. The temperature was always pleasant in the room, even if his hosts were not. In the back corner, barely visible, was a small bar and a single bar dog standing behind it. Johnson did not know the man's name. He believed their good stock was kept back here. He had heard that a few of the barons even drank wine as opposed to liquor. He remembered hearing once that wine was not a drink but a food. It seemed as stupid then as now. Johnson was always amazed that the barons had not upgraded their den with an overhead or even electricity. They all could well afford it.

The lamp gave little glow, and Johnson's eyes were accustomed to the outside light. Still, he could make out the usual group of four or five men in hundred-dollar suits sitting around the only table in there. The table was nicer than the ones in the saloon and always looked new. Whenever the barons gathered, there was a game. He did not take time to look at the cards to see what it was today. He had never been asked to stay too long on his reporting visits and always wondered what the rest of the room might reveal. Harmonson swung his hand, motioning him inside to his customary position, a few feet back from the table and facing the barons. He guessed he always stood in the vacancy where Harmonson had been sitting, as he always remained standing behind him during his calls. Truth was they probably didn't let Harmonson sit either.

"What do we owe the pleasure, Marshal?" the one farthest from him asked.

"I received a telegram concerning rustlers in the Indian Territory.

I believe it may lead us to solve the problem up there," Johnson replied. He was nervous and his mouth tasted like parchment.

"What did it say?" another asked.

"That the ring is headed by the Marlow gang, probably located around the Fort Sill area," Johnson said. Johnson was a liar. There was no "ring" or "gang" and he knew it, but an arrest and conviction of these Marlow horse thieves would show the barons he could do his job. And who knew, the Marlows might be some ringleaders, there could be a gang.

"And when are you going after this *gang?*" the one farthest from him asked.

"I plan on leaving first light as soon as I can get a few of the fellers to go with me." The man farthest from him stood up slowly. As he walked over to Johnson, he even appeared to be smiling through the smoke of his own cigar. He came over and placed his arm around the marshal. Then he laughed and patted him on the back again. He laughed so hard that the others in the room began laughing as well. Johnson thought he must have missed a joke and, not wanting to appear rude, joined in. When the big man saw him laughing, he hawed even harder and had to stop to wipe a tear from his eye.

Still smiling and rubbing Johnson's shoulder, he looked him in the eyes. "Listen, you one-armed jackass. If you, and whoever the devil you choose to deputize, are not riding north out of town by dusk, I'll personally cut your other arm off. *Sabe?*" Johnson had quit smiling, but the baron maintained his genial demeanor throughout. All the marshal could muster was a humbled "Yessir," and he backed out of the room. The man patted him on the back one last time and returned to his seat. Once on the other side of the door, Harmonson stuck his face out, looked either way, reached out, squeezed the marshal's one good arm, smiled, and said, "Why, Ed, ain't you the charmer. Better hurry on now, or you will have to find someone to help you wipe your arse."

CHAPTER 4

―――・✦・―――

WILD HORSE CREEK
INDIAN TERRITORY

*M*artha Jane Marlow kept a tidy home and she hoped a Godly one as well. She certainly didn't care for the name of the community they lived in, even though she found the title appropriate. The place was certainly wild. It hadn't been easy with five sons and a daughter she had raised almost by herself, or so it remembered that way. Her late husband had been a physician but spent most of his time looking for gold that wasn't there, from California to Colorado, and even for a spell in Mexico. Now he was dead and her family financially no further along, following that same nomadic spirit of the trail that had gripped America since its beginnings. Only the trail now was gold or cattle. They had never been too sharp with the gold, but cattle were different. Here in south central Indian Territory, they kept a nice herd of fifty or so cow and calf. And it was here that the wayfaring life would soon end; the territory was going to open up to settlers in a few months and each stake of land would be practically given to the people who were the first to claim it. Marlow grass. That was Martha Jane's plan . . . God, her family, and their own land.

God was always there for her and she saw to it, as she believed He did, that the land would soon follow. Her whole earthly focus in life was her five sons: George, Boone, Alfred, Lewellyn, and Charley. Her daughter was married and she had entrusted her to the girl's husband. George had stepped into his father's authority, and when he did not assume the mantle, Charley would. They were the oldest, with Boone the baby. None of them was a hair over five foot five and none would weigh 150 pounds soaking wet. All had learned early that their small stature was an impediment to life on the frontier and had developed attitudes to make up for it.

She had wanted grandchildren to spoil, but there were none yet. Her daughter was the only one married, and her husband was a stock farmer in Vernon, Texas—just across the Red River. Boone was her only son who had taken to a girl so far. Her name was Susan Harboldt, and she was comely, but as far as Martha Jane was concerned, white trash. She lived with her two brothers a few miles away from the Marlow dugout on Hell Roaring Creek, and the boys were always in trouble with the law. She did not know what had happened to the girl's parents, but put nothing past her brothers. She had finally forbidden Boone to court her further.

She put aside her things and walked outside to enjoy what remained of the morning. The heat would soon arrive and the sky would turn white in the afternoon. It was coming later and later as fall approached—and that was a blessing. There was no way to determine the seasons on the southern plains, except for the changes in temperature and the drives. They happened at the same time every year in the early fall and late spring. Her boys would leave again just like they did every year, and every year she would worry anew. She tried to turn all her worries over to God, though she felt it was her right as a mother to be concerned. The trail was a dangerous place and the cow towns worse.

Standing in the door, she noticed a group of riders approaching from the west on the Fort Sill road. They rarely had company. She believed firmly in offering any help she could to strangers; the Good Book said they could always be angels. Martha Jane Marlow was not about to offend any angels, and she quoted aloud Hebrews 13:2, "Be not forgetful to entertain strangers for thereby some have entertained angels unawares." She went back into the dugout to warm up what was left of breakfast and put on some fresh coffee. They were probably drovers looking for work before the fall roundups. She couldn't offer any work, though she could fill their bellies. Besides, the next time it might be her boys away from home, and she always prayed that folks might be there to help them if they needed.

The coffee had just started to boil when she heard the horses rein up outside. She quickly took her apron off and patted her hair to ensure it wasn't mussed. She walked out to greet her visitors. The men were covered with the trail and their horses looked spent. Two of the men were dismounted and checking the hoofs and cinches of their mounts. A man with one arm remained ahorse and smiled and took off his hat when Martha Jane came out on the front porch. The man sitting next to him just stared, and the one-armed man hit him with his hat and motioned toward the lady. The saddle bum blushed and removed his hat.

"Well, howdy, gentlemen. I don't have much to offer, but I can fetch some fatback on the stove and the coffee is hot."

"Thankee, ma'am. But we will have to pass on the victuals. Could we trouble you for some fresh water for our mounts? We have been riding through the night."

"Why, surely. Just help yourselves. The trough is over by the corral, and we might have some grain as well." The men appeared friendly enough; still, she had an unpleasant feeling about them. Maybe they would just water and leave. They seemed to be heavily armed for drovers. The one-armed man dismounted, as did the rest. He gave his horse to one of the other men, who took it along with the others to water. He moved up to the doorway.

"Obliged for the water, ma'am, but we ain't needin' no grain. We are looking to hire some boys for a drive and heard you had sons that might want the work. But I believe I have been misinformed—you must be their sister. I do not believe a lady as pretty as yourself could have dammed one son, let alone five. Are your brothers around?" Marshal Johnson had grown accustomed to lying and had even gotten good at it. He had learned to smile, say please, tip his hat, and concoct stories to throw off people. Martha Jane felt disarmed by the man's pleasantness and took pity on him for his missing arm.

"Well, mister..." Martha Jane was blushing and she knew it. Vanity was a sin. She could not help being flattered and brushed back her hair just a bit from her eyes. She was just a little embarrassed over the plain gray dress she had worn for many years. Rarely had any man taken a notice of her since her husband's passing.

"I am Ed Johnson, ma'am. I work for the Bar C Ranch down in Young County, Texas." Johnson felt comfortable in giving his own name and where he was really from. It heightened the stakes and made the hunt more interesting.

"Mister Johnson, I do have five sons and they might be interested in your work. Elly and Boone are over in that field gathering corn, and Charley and Alf are up digging potatoes for an Indian chief named Sun Boy up around Fort Sill. My eldest, George, works for him as well, and he stops in when his duties for the chief allow."

Johnson thanked her for her time and the fresh water and moved to join the men at the trough. Once there, he spoke to them for a moment, then they all mounted and turned toward the field where Boone and Elly were gathering corn. The field was about a half-mile from the cabin, and Martha Jane kept her face turned toward them the entire time as they approached her two boys.

Boone and Elly had been at work for nearly four hours straight, and it wasn't even noon yet. August had always been the hottest of months, and today there was no breeze to cool them off. The field did not even appear to have a dent in it for all their labors this morning. They had brought the buckboard and team over with them.

"Dern, Boone, I can still see the wood on the bottom of the wagon," Elly said as he stopped for a moment and leaned against the frame.

"Mama will make you see stars in your head if she catches ya loafin'."

"I ain't *loafin'*, jus' catching my breath is all," Elly snapped back. He had seen the men stop at the dugout and take on water but had given it no concern. Instead of the men riding on the road, they had detoured over to the cornfield and were riding straight at the two brothers. "Hey, Boone, yonder come them fellers Mama was talking at. Wonder if they is looking for drovers?"

"Land, I hope so. I was not made to be no boomer." Boone kept on shucking the corn and didn't even look at the men until they had ridden upon them. The men had stopped just short of the boys and formed a semicircle around them. Boone looked up from his chores, and Elly shaded his eyes so he could see them. All at once, the men pulled iron and drew down on the two.

"Hands up!" Johnson shouted. The brothers did not know what to do. No one had ever told them that before, and they blankly returned his stare.

"Hands up." Again the brothers felt awkward and embarrassed more than afraid, and neither moved.

"I said hands up, or so help me I will gun you down where you stand." Johnson punctuated the remark by cocking his pistol. The rest of his men followed the action. Whatever the dialogue had done, the cocking put a sense of urgency into the boys, and both shot up their hands immediately.

"We ain't done nothing wrong, mister," Elly said.

"I am U.S. Marshal Ed Johnson, and you are under arrest for

rustling. You boys hop in the back of that wagon and clear out that corn." The brothers did what they were told. After they cleared the corn out of the wagon, one of the posse dismounted and shackled the two together in the bed.

Martha Jane had not felt comfortable during the pleasantries and cursed herself for being so flattered that she let her guard down. As soon as the men had drawn their weapons, she moved as fast as her legs could go out to the field. By the time she arrived, her two sons were manacled and sitting humbly in the back of the wagon. Two men had tethered their horses to the rear of it and were in the seat, turning the buckboard out of the field and onto the road. Johnson saw Martha Jane at the last minute and moved his horse in front of her to block the way.

"You know what your thieving sons have done. We are taking them to the agency, and you cannot go near them. Do you understand?"

"I have started to my boys, and God help me, I shall do so even if it costs me my life." She stared at the deputy and stepped around his animal. She was afraid and angry. She had shown these men hospitality, and they repaid her by drawing guns on her property.

As soon as she made it to the wagon, one of the mounted men clubbed her in the breast with the butt of his rifle. It wasn't too hard, but she didn't see it coming, and the blow knocked her down to the ground. Both boys jerked to the side of the wagon their mother was near.

"Mama!" Boone screamed. Johnson had turned his horse too late to stop the blow. He winced when he saw the lady hit but was not about to let two prisoners escape. He jerked his pistol and leveled it on the two, who seemed bound to get to their mother.

"First one out of that wagon will die as sure as I am sitting here." The brothers both glared back at him; the youngest was starting to cry.

"Just sit yourselves back in that buckboard and everything will be all right." Johnson motioned to his deputy. "Pick up the lady and help her into the dugout. Boys, I am sorry that happened." Both brothers met his stare, and Johnson noticed that it wasn't fear that was making the youth cry—it was rage.

The posse member took Martha Jane and put her on the bed. She was shaky and for a few minutes did not seem to remember who they were or what had transpired. One of the more sensitive deputies even placed a damp cloth on her forehead so she would be more comfortable.

The wagon with the brothers pulled up in front of the cabin, and Johnson gave the order for the property to be searched for firearms and stolen goods. All that was found were a couple of firearms and no evidence of stolen property. Johnson, satisfied that nothing else remained, turned his group back onto the road south. As they were pulling away from the cabin, Martha Jane stepped out, holding on to the doorjamb for support.

"Where are you taking my sons?"

Johnson rode his horse forward to speak.

"Madam, I am sorry about what happened to you. I never meant that."

"Where are you taking my sons?"

"To the Fort Sill Agency just west of here." With that, she disappeared back inside. Johnson shrugged and moved his men onto the road. As they were clearing the property, he noticed that Martha Jane Marlow, walking some distance behind and holding the damp cloth against her head, had joined his procession.

One-quarter mile out of Sill, the marshal stopped the procession. The thought occurred that that prisoners should walk the remaining distance into town. It just felt right to Johnson—no need to let these townspeople see them in a decent light, in the back of a wagon. That was too respectable; let them be seen for the criminals they were.

Later in the evening, Martha Jane stumbled up to the buckboard. Her sons had already been bedded down inside the agency jail on Fort Sill. She was not allowed inside by the jailer, who wondered why the woman was so filthy and disheveled. He referred her to Agent White's office down the street. She went to the office, found Johnson, and argued until he took her to her sons. Johnson said little along the way. He picked up his pace so nobody would think he was with a crazy woman.

Once inside the jail, she saw Elly, Boone, and her other two sons, Alf and Charley, but not George. Johnson must have had men ride to Sun Boy's ranch to apprehend them as well. She did the best she could to take away their concerns about her. She was fine and would be better after a little rest. Johnson told her the boys were being taken to Young County, Texas, to stand trial for rustling. She did not argue, only asked when he would be leaving and did she have time to bring them some fresh clothes. Johnson would leave in the morning; she could take the wagon and come back again before he left. Her sons agreed.

Her trip out and back to Wild Horse Creek had taken all night. She had packed what food she could and gotten as much of their traps together as time allowed. She thought about taking her poke but did not. She would not need it. The boys were going to be fine and they would obey the law. This would be over in no time.

She arrived back at Sill before daybreak and parked the wagon in front of the jail. She would ask the jailer to help her unload. She saw no reason to knock and went into the building. The room was empty and no lawman was present. She walked down the hall and saw that the cells were empty too. She stopped for a moment and grabbed the bars; her heart fluttered just a bit. Her sons had already been taken away from her.

CHAPTER 5

*T*he environs were not too different from a cattle drive except for the absence of a chuck and Mary. The area they stopped in was good bunch ground, as good as any the brothers had ever seen. The horses were hobbled, and the jingle of the bell mare could be heard just outside of the camp. The smells of mesquite fire, beef, horse dung, and Arbuckle's saturated and mixed together in the air. The men were all dressed for the trail, except for the brothers, who were still in their shirtsleeves. Once over the ford, the posse stopped for the night on a bluff overlooking the Red. The river was low and the crossing had been easy. An acorn calf with a blab board still in its nose had been stuck in some mud on a sandbar, and as they passed near him one of the posse threw a hoolihan over his head and dragged him out. Once he was out, they butchered the animal and ate him mostly raw after he had cooked some over a fire.

There was only one fire, and that was for the deputies. The coriente beef and the smell of mesquite stirred up all of the insects that infested riverbanks. The brothers were still shackled but at least had been allowed to get out of the wagon before they were chained to a spoke. They were not permitted any of the calf and soothed their bellies, angry with the smell of fresh beef, with a few leftover corn shucks that remained in the wagon. The heavy smoke from the fire protected the deputies from the insects but gave little cover to the brothers.

Boone began to talk again. He had not been born with the mechanism in his head to decipher problems in his gut, so anything he thought about, he talked about. He was known all over the central territory as a flannel-mouth and had kept a steady flow all the way to the Red and even commented on the deputy's roping ability with the steer. Once they discovered a few shucks in the buckboard, he gobbled his portion and began to talk again. The energy he drew from the raw corn did him right, and he commented on the bugs, on the deputies, on who would get the peppermint at the bottom of the coffee bag, and over and over asked why they were under arrest.

"Shut up, Boone," Charley said. Boone was also incapable of hiding his emotions and shot a hurt stare at his older brother.

"I was just talkin' to pass the time, Charley," Boone responded.

"Yeah, well, I am sick of your gas and it ain't helping anybody, so just shut up and let me think."

"Ma says—"

"Ma ain't here, Boone, and neither is George, and Daddy is dead, so just hush and let me think." Boone sat sour-faced and looked down. After a few minutes he fished around in his shirt pocket and pulled a Durham sack with his makings and began to roll one. He held the papers gingerly in his fingers and poured the tobacco down the center, licked it, and completed a roll. Once the smoke was in his mouth, he leaned back and took a pack of lucifers from his pants pocket. As he lit the cigarette he noticed all of his brothers staring a hole through him with shocked looks on their faces. Boone shook out the match.

"Well, you told me to stop gabbin'."

"Boone, if Mama were to catch you, she'd beat the tar out of ya," Elly said.

"Well, like big brother says," Boone said, letting out the drag, "she ain't here."

The brothers and most of the deputies were asleep. A north wind blew, and they were chilled but did not have the blankets to spare for their prisoners. The sleep was fitful at best, and Boone drifted in his mind back to his last trouble.

James Holdson had just left a well-stocked saloon in Vernon and rode out to his assignment. He had been hired by the stockmen to clear out the postage-stamp operations that were dividing up his employer's ranches. He was feeling the warm glow of his indulgence as he rode up to the Gilmore homestead. Once in front, he stepped off, nearly lost his balance, regained it, and moved to the front door. Elizabeth Gilmore answered the knock and then called for her husband. Holdson stood in the door frame, one hand on his gun and the other hanging on the jamb, all horns and cattle. He called them "nesters," and his questions were reckless and without sense, though they sounded sane to Holdson.

Boone had just left his brothers in the territory and meant to spend a few days with his sister in Vernon. As he neared the home, he eyed his sister and her husband on the front porch talking with a large man Boone did not know, but from the looks of him he guessed he was a dreg looking for cow work.

As Boone got closer, his sister and her husband went back inside the cabin, but the man stayed on the porch. As soon as he got within fifty yards of the house, the man drew his sidearm and began firing at Boone. Boone was never a shot from a horse and although confused by the man's behavior, passed on questioning him, dismounted, and pulled his Winchester from its sleeve and fired a single shot through Holdson's heart. The man's expression did not change, nor did he grab his chest. He just went limp, collapsed, and died. Boone recollected later he fell like a rag doll.

Boone walked over to the body as his sister and her husband ran out of the house and out into the yard near the pair. Boone had never seen a dead man before and noticed how quickly a circle of red mud grew in the dirt. The way the liquid spread reminded Boone of an egg cracked from its shell and spreading on a hot skillet. It kept getting wider until it threatened to overtake Boone's boots. He stepped back out of its way and wondered how much blood a person could hold. On the outer circle, the mud was almost black and got lighter toward the man until just at the edge of him you could see its true color. He thought he was supposed to feel something bad but didn't, and that bothered him.

"Oh, Boone, what have you done?

"In God's name, sis, who is that man and why did he want to kill me?"

"He came asking questions and was half drunk too. He must have mistaken you for someone else."

"Well, it was a bad mistake. What shall we do?"

Boone's brother-in-law was standing over Holdson. "I will notify the sheriff. You were perfectly justified in shooting him, Boone, but there is no telling what trouble may result. You had better seek safety."

And then Boone was falling, and all he could concentrate on during the fall was that if he did not wake up before he hit the ground, he would die. Boone jerked up from his sleep. At first he thought he was on a drive with his brothers until he reached up to rub his eyes and remembered the shackles. His thoughts were clouded from the doze. Then he began to piece it together. After he had killed the man, he had immediately set out for Colorado and did not come home until his family sent for him. There had never been any more talk of it, and Boone had let it pass from his mind.

He did not believe the charge of rustling they were accused of. He was being arrested for the killing of that cowboy at his sister's place some years before. What if these men were friends of that fellow, or worse, they believed all the Marlow clan were involved? He wished George were here and then took the wish back; he was glad George was free and could look after their ma. He just wished he knew what George would want him to do. Oh, dear Lord, what if they hanged all of his brothers for his sin? It just would not do. He had wanted to stay when it had happened, but his family made him leave the territory. He would right things at once.

He glanced at his sleeping brothers. If they woke and caught on, they would prevent him from saving them. He was fifty feet from the deputies and would wake the camp if he hallooed out. Just then he saw the lone guard checking the hobbled horses just at the rim of the fire's light. He waved his hand and coughed, but the man paid no attention. He remembered his tobacco sack, and though he hated to part with it, tossed it and hit the deputy on the John B.

Boone, with his brothers still shackled and asleep, found himself with a plateful of beef and sitting cross-legged in front of the marshal and some of the waked posse.

Johnson reviewed his notes. "So you kilt this fellow... uh, Holdson, with one shot." The marshal seemed impressed as Boone continued spewing the details of his manslaughter. He felt a bit guilty at first and only relented to eating after the marshal agreed to feed his brothers likewise in the morning.

"Yes sir, stepped off my hoss, and shot him dead through the heart."

"Any papers on ya?"

"No, sir, never heard of any."

"Did ya notch yer gun?" one of the more eager posse asked.

"No. No I did not. I just killed him, that is all. I took no pride in it." Boone seemed surprised by the question.

Deputy Marshal Johnson found himself in the best mood in months. Not only had he captured a gang of thieves, he got a murderer to boot. There had to be paper on him. As soon as they returned to Young County, a trip to Vernon was in order. Might be some reward as well. This would show the barons that he was doing their job.

PART II

SEPTEMBER–DECEMBER 1888

CHAPTER 6

ANADARKO AGENCY
INDIAN TERRITORY

*I*t had taken two days for the riders to find George. Sun Boy had dispatched them as soon as the posse arrested Alf and Charley. George was well liked by all the chief's people, and the braves went to find him. He was on his way back from Colorado, where he had taken care of Sun Boy's affairs, and had settled in for the night on a creek a day's ride from his home. The riders came in fast and did not "halloo" from the trail, just rode in and gave George a start.

The story had to be repeated to him twice before the sleep wore down and he began to grasp his family's trouble. The sleep faded. He saddled up Shoat in the dark, nodded his thanks at the messengers, and rode off.

At first George did not know which way to go, then remembered Agent White's name mentioned by the bucks. He reined Shoat off the road and headed for the agent's office at Sill.

The ride took the rest of the night. He pulled into the main street of Sill and rode straight over to the agent's office. The night was still present and the chill of dawn came over both George and Shoat. Shoat was wet and shivered a bit. No one was on the streets. The post commander had regulated a curfew since some soldiers had shot up a saloon.

George tethered Shoat and walked up to the window of the agent's office. His breath fogged up the pane and he cupped his hands to see inside. He could just make out the sounds of snoring. He tapped on the window and the nasal drone stopped and faltered, then continued just the same. George went over to the door, drew his pistol, and rapped the heel several times on the jamb. He listened, and the snoring had been replaced with swearing like that he had heard the last time he was in this office. The oaths were angered and self-righteous. A candle's light peeked from under the door in the office, and Agent White's shadow came through it. He was wearing his nightshirt and smoking cap, holding the lantern and feeling his way toward the office door. The latch moved, and White pulled open the door. He stared confused at his visitor and held up the lantern in his left hand to George's face. The sleep faded and was replaced by recognition, then a smile.

"Mr. Marlow," White said.

"Yes, sir."

Agent White placed the pepperbox in his right hand under George's nose. Calmly and with no malice.

"Nice to see you again. You are under arrest, for horse thievery."

Four days later, George was released. Agent White had telegraphed Marshal Johnson and received no word. George learned that his brothers were charged with rustling and they were being held in Young County, Texas. In the mean, Sun Boy had been causing a stir among the Indians and Anglos. A widow woman being abused by Texas lawmen had not set well. Some army officers from the fort were nosing around too. As soon as word got out, people who wouldn't have given any of the Marlows a second glance on the street were coming by and demanding he be charged or released. Some Yankee Jew lawyer had started asking questions, using words Agent White could not even pronounce. Reluctantly, White released George Marlow. George found Shoat in the livery and paid his bill; though he did not think he should be liable, he did not have the time to waste on an argument.

It took two days to reach his mother. Sun Boy's braves had loaded all the Marlows' possessions on wagons and had escorted Mother Marlow and their stock to the north bank of the Red to wait on George. George thanked the braves, but they would not take their leave until George had the wagons and remuda across the river. Mother Marlow was under a shebang built alongside the buckboard. She sat in her porch chair with her poke in her lap. She looked upon George as the prodigal, and began weeping. George was taken aback. Through all the challenges, deaths, and crises, he had never seen his mother cry. She did not rise to greet him, only bowed her head in her hands and thanked God.

George calmed her as best he could. She settled some and withdrew her Bible from her poke. George ranged around and began coaling the fire to prepare a meal for them and the bucks. They would leave in the morning. His mother began reading her Bible out loud. It was a psalm George had never heard before.

"But those that seek my soul, to destroy it, shall go into the lower parts of the earth. They shall fall by the sword; they shall be a portion for foxes. But the king shall rejoice in God; everyone that sweareth by him shall glory; but the mouth of them that speak lies shall be stopped."

CHAPTER 7

YOUNG COUNTY JAIL
GRAHAM, TEXAS

The jailer was slow in getting to the door. George had left his mother on the Brazos and had ridden into town by himself. Their trip had been smooth but had taken over a week. Just outside of Graham, George found a couple of Indians camped nearby, and they told him where the jail was. The knob turned, and George worried over whether to give his real name. The door opened a crack, and the light from a lantern and blistering heat came through.

"What is it?" A dirty little man still in his work clothes said, still rubbing the sleep out of his eyes with the heel of his hand.

"I am George Marlow. I came to see my brothers and am unarmed and alone." The dirty jailer nodded his head and opened the door with apparently no thought to caution. For all he knew, George was here to break his brothers out. He was either sleepy or dull or both. George nodded his thanks and stepped inside.

The jailer said nothing, just turned down the hallway and motioned for George to follow. They went past the administrative office and past the private quarters to the stairs. The jailer motioned with the lantern up the stairs and turned toward his room.

"They is up there. I got the keys and a gun and am going back to bed. You can show yourself out." He handed George the candle and walked toward his door, scratching. George was in mild shock and did not know what to do.

"Obliged. Good night," George said. The jailer kept walking and waved over his head and closed the door. For a moment, it all felt like a dream. There was George, after midnight, in Texas, about to visit his four brothers in jail, left unsupervised by a crazy jailer. George shrugged and walked up the stairs.

At the landing, he opened the steel door and stepped through into an anteroom with another steel door, opened it, and poked his head through into the dark. He smelled sweat and urine from the chamber pots and unbathed men. The sounds of sleep were mild compared to what his brothers were capable of. What if he was in the wrong jail? The sign out front had read "County," but he was pretty sure they were under federal charges. He brought the candle around the door to light the room.

As soon as the flame caught George's face, a familliar voice said, "Took you long enough, big brother."

George stepped into the room, squinted, and followed the sound of his brother's voice. "Charley?" he called. There were only two cells, one on either side of the room. The cells themselves were large and were obviously intended to hold groups. There was a wide passageway in between. His brother's voice came from the cell on his right. George held up the candle and showed the bars with his next younger brother, unshaven, red-eyed, and filthy, looking at him. George threw up the candle to light the other cells.

"Do not bother. We are all in here. Just some drunks in the far one."

"Shet yer pie-hole, hoss thief, afore I shet it fer ye." One of the "drunks" did not like being called such. George started to reply, but Charlie interrupted.

"Do not bother, he has passed back out again most likely. Come over here and take my hand." George smiled and grabbed his brother through the bars, and both gave their best at a hug and pats on the back.

"It is good to see you well and here. How is Mama?"

"She is worried and tired but otherwise fine. We have a camp out on the Brazos and have brought the remuda. We had to abandon the dugout and pray it is safe kept while we are down here. What is your status, and when can we get you out of here?"

"It will not be easy. Charges are federal and for rustling. Marshal Johnson was the one what arrested us, and his office, they tell me, is just west across the town's square in the federal court building. We came in at night, so I cannot vouch for sure. The county sheriff, Wallace, has been taking care of us. Wallace is a good man and does not care for Johnson. It was probably Joe Leavell that let you in. He is the jailer and harmless, though an idiot."

"I noticed that."

George and Charles spoke for the next hour before they both agreed that he had better get back to tend to Mother Marlow.

The pecan trees along the salt fork of the Brazos River provided George and his mother's camp some shade, and they were pitched above the flood line. For the past few days, George had been going in every other day to visit his brothers and take them some food. George had retained a mouthpiece, and Martha Jane's spirits were greatly improved. The lawyer had told them that bond would soon be set, and the brothers could be free awaiting the trial. George had even struck up something of a friendship with the county sheriff, Wallace, though he thought the deputy, Tom Collier, a bully. He had yet to eye the one-armed federal marshal Johnson, whom his mother said was to blame for all this.

George was cutting some wood and heard a horse stop at the wagon. He walked around the side and saw Collier, on a horse, speaking to his mother.

"Hidy, Tom, light and sit with us." George was annoyed at his presence, yet thought better of being belligerent.

"No. I will have to pull you," Collier said, looking away and making no eye contact with George or his mother. Mother Marlow started after Collier, and George stepped between the two.

"What for?"

"That is the orders of Ed." George knew he meant the one-armed federal officer.

"Where are your papers?"

"Ed has them."

"I thought you worked for Sheriff Wallace. If this is federal business, why are you here?"

Collier looked back at George and did not offer a reason. He wiped at his nose and looked back toward the road, then at George. George had enough.

"I will come in the morning." And George turned back to his work.

"No, come in now, Ed is out there," Collier said motioning up toward the road.

George nodded and saddled Shoat. He kissed his mother and hitched up the buckboard for her so she could go into town with them. He told her to get to the lawyer's office and see to their bail.

Martha Jane had not gone into town until today and had forgotten what a busy town looked like. She drove the buckboard through the streets. George had mentioned that the lawyer's office was on the west side of the square near the federal courthouse. Once on the square, she got her bearings and was relieved that she would not have to drive past the saloons and sporting houses on the north side.

She thought better than to visit her boys in jail. She knew her heart could not bear it. Her focus must be on their liberty, not incarceration. She turned the team and caught sight of the federal court. Coming out was Ed Johnson, who had not seen her. He turned and walked south down the boardwalk checking his timepiece and swatting at flies. Martha Jane slacked the reins and drove up behind him. He either did not hear or ignored the wagon. Martha waited until she was alongside the marshal.

"Afternoon, Marshal."

"Afternoon, m'a...." Johnson stopped. He had intentionally stayed out of their camp earlier to avoid a confrontation, and now he had one right here in downtown Graham. Wouldn't look good in the paper to have another scene like what had happened in the IT. Johnson tipped his hat and continued walking, only just a bit faster.

"You are a black liar, and my boys are innocent of the crimes you have arrested them for." The passersby had slowed some and were watching the drama. Graham was busy but also boring; any intrigues would be well received and talked of incessantly. Johnson moved quicker, trying to ignore her and nodding greetings at the constituents. Martha Jane, realizing she had an attentive audience and a productive situation, increased her fervor.

"I prayed for you last night, for God to forgive you and give you the strength to recant your ways. God will judge harshly your attentions on a widow and her innocent children." As the procession moved along, more and more people followed and listened. All Johnson could do was cut across Oak Street over to the county courthouse and duck inside. He quickly jumped in front of the team and quickened his pace. Martha Jane stopped the wagon and watched him scurry over to the building. She was never one to make a scene, but having just made one, took some satisfaction in it. The citizens were still milling near the buckboard on the sidewalk, and Martha Jane felt one final comment was needed.

"Justice is God's will and the devil's yoke." She punctuated the statement by slapping the reins and driving over to the lawyer's shingle.

George had taken over his father's role, and Martha Jane had little interest in the details of man's law. Now, with all her boys in jail, she found herself with no choice. There was no friendly chime-ring when she opened the door. The legal office was typical of what she had imagined. The room smelled of old books and money. It was laid out as if a courtroom—a small waiting area with a rail section dividing it in two and the main room. The lawyer's desk was set higher than the rest of the room, so as someone stood before it they would have to look up to see the person seated behind the bench. The bench, what Martha Jane could see of it, was piled high with papers, in no particular order, it seemed. Behind the papers was a bald head, and Martha Jane was suddenly struck by a vision of Ebenezer Scrooge, and Bob Cratchit about to ask him for Christmas Day off. Martha Jane had less use for fiction than for man's jurisprudence. Even so, that story had been a favorite, since it dealt with God's basic plan of repentance and redemption.

Martha Jane made a small *ahem* to get the head's attention. Perhaps George had gone to a different lawyer, or he had storied and had not gone to one at all. The bald head did not move. Martha Jane did not have the time to be patient. Then the head spoke.

"Yes, ma'am. You must be the boy's mother. I understand, er, um, George was just arrested this morning. Terrible, terrible."

"Yes, sir. I am the boy's mother, Martha Jane Marlow." She felt that at least one of them must offer an introduction. There was no reason to be immediately familiar with the man. "We have remitted your five hundred dollars. George was arrested this morning, and I came here to find out what you intend to do about it."

The head was taken aback a bit. "Forgive me, madam. My name is Robert Arnold, and, er, um, yes, well… what to do about it; that is a bit of a trick, now, I mean to tell you."

"Mr. Arnold, I am sure I do not understand. We have paid you a significant cash advance that we could not even afford. The question is simple. What are you planning on for my boys?"

"Um, yes, well, the charge against your sons is quite serious and we must proceed with caution. Now—"

"Mr. Arnold, I… *we* do not have time to proceed with caution. My whole family is in your jail and the boys as innocent in this matter as Job. Our homestead is vacant and liable for harm; we have crops due in and must return to the territories. Now, what do you intend to do?"

The head stared at her over the piles. 'Very well, madam. How much property do you have with you in Young County?"

"Just now?"

"Yes, ma'am, just now."

"We have the buckboard and a small remuda. Some furniture a tent and camp utensils as well."

"Do you know anyone here in town who may be able to forward you an advance?"

Martha Jane felt her lip quiver, "No, sir. Not just yet. We . . . I have only been in town two weeks, and people aren't so able to befriend someone whose entire family is in the local jail."

Arnold nodded, "Yes, quite." He seemed lost for a moment, reached over into a bowl, took out a wet rag, and dabbed it around his bald head even though the fall weather was mild. "Madam, I will be able to secure bail for your sons, but you must have a means to pay for it. What I mean is, er, um, I urge you to sell all your remuda and conveyance and we may be able to raise enough money to free one or more of your sons."

"One or more . . . goodness, how am I supposed to decide which one gets free and which remains imprisoned? How could I do that Mr. Arnold?"

"Perhaps the boys could draw straws or likewise—it does not matter just now, madam. What matters is you liquidating your assets so we may approach the court. This is a federal matter and is likely to be expensive. You might also consider some place for employment for yourself and your sons as they get released. Perhaps on one of the local farms or ranches, though that may prove problematic considering the charges against your sons. Foxes guarding the hens, so to speak—oh, no offense, ma'am."

Martha Jane sighed, "None taken, Mr. Arnold. I will go to the livery and do what I can. I will be back in touch with you on the morrow. Good day."

The head stood up and walked around the bench. *Well,* Martha Jane thought, *at least he has some manners. Certainly uses big words.* He took her arm and escorted her to the door. "And good day to you, ma'am. Robert Arnold is on the case." He held the door, and Martha Jane nodded politely and stepped out, climbed up into the seat, released the brake, and drove off to the livery.

She stirred up the team and turned north. It saddened her that the livery was on the same row as the bawdy houses, and she hoped no one recognized her. Their reputations were soiled enough by the charges, and they did not need any help from busybodies spreading lies about the boys' mother on the wrong side of the square.

In her opinion, and she prayed God forgive her for it, Texans were a worthless sort. Every experience she had in the state had been for the worst. Her husband died. Boone killed a saddle bum. No good ever came from south of the Red. She was sure there must have been some Christians living here, but as of yet she had not met any.

She reined up at the Boyles & Kramer Livery. "Horses stabled, bought and sold," the sign read. She braked and stepped down. Next to the entrance was an old man wearing denim and sitting on a bench with a towheaded boy picking his nose. Martha Jane shot the boy a stare and considered scolding him when the old man spoke up, "Do not mind him, his head is messed up. In a minute, I reckon, he will eat one or two boogers if you keep watching him like that."

"Yes, well, bless his heart, then. Are you the proprietor?"

"Are you looking for a livery for the night?"

"No. I have a small remuda for sale and I need to talk business with someone in charge."

"'At's too bad. The rates is right decent. Won't find any better," the old man said, slapping the boy's hand before he could ingest anything.

"Thank you, no." Martha Jane was impatient. "Is there someone I may talk business to, sir?"

The old man sniffed and stood up slowly, grabbing the rail of the bench to help himself to vertical. "Follow me, ma'am." Martha Jane looked to ensure that the brake was in its place and followed the old man into the livery.

It turned out the owner was the old man's son and the boy's father. She did not inquire after the child, and assumed that problems must have occurred because of a fever, as he appeared physically sound. The owner was quite professional and businesslike. So much so that Martha Jane felt sad, for surely the man realized that his surrounding bloodlines gave no assistance to good business. He did not have the cloak of ignorance that the Good Lord provided to those in need. Nevertheless, he seemed to accept his situation and be happy about it. He would ride out to her camp in the morning and set his price. Martha Jane thanked him, bid him good day, and took her leave back to the camp.

The cells may have held two or three comfortably, if that was not obscene, but five was intolerable. The boys were all the more worried for their mother, now that George was not able to care for her. The door to the room opened, and Joe Leavell, the turnkey who had let George in some weeks before, carried in the dinner meal in the dinner bucket, so noted because the sheriff had painted the bucket for each meal a different color. Blue for breakfast, et cetera. It did not ensure that the buckets would be well cleaned in between victuals, only that the previous meal would not be caked on outside the edges. Wallace felt that was the best he could do.

Sheriff Wallace followed Leavell in. Wallace leaned against the cells opposite while the turnkey scooped the stew up and poured it into the cups the prisoners held through the bars. Leavell, as was his custom, said nothing and did not make eye contact. Just looked at the floor, sniffed, and scooped. When he was finished, he turned and walked past Wallace and out the door. The boys, except George, began eating.

"Why ain't you eating your stew, son?" Wallace walked over to their cell and took hold of the bars, being careful to keep his sidearm on the away side. He felt that these men were innocent of these particular charges and smelled the chance to show Johnson as an ass, but men under duress were liable to do anything. There was never any way to be sure.

"I guess I am not hungry, trying too hard to think. The food will not go to waste."

"No doubt. Is y'all's mama going to be all right?" Wallace ran his fingers around the joint of the bars. Unlike Johnson, he made eye contact with the boys, was friendly, and seemed genuinely concerned for their mother.

"Don't know. Mama is pretty tough, but this is not home either," Charley answered in between bites.

"I'll have my wife over to check on her. We take in boarders, though I do not think it would be a good idea to have your mother in. There is a rancher in between here and Jacksboro in a town called Finis that may be able to help some." The boys, except for George, stopped eating and looked at him.

"What do you mean help?" George asked, beginning to eye his plate with some hunger.

"Just what I said help. He has a small cottage that he rents out for labor around his place. His property is not too big, but it winds all around the Brazos and is hard for him to take care of. Not bad if you don't mind tote and fetch for a work-a-day. Your mother could probably stay there, and as bail is raised you boys could join her and earn your keep until the trial."

The boys all looked at each other and then all at George.

"When could this happen, Sheriff?" George replied.

"My wife can tell your mama tomorrow, and I will help her get moved myself." The boys did not reply. They were shocked by the offer. No one had offered them any help since this had all begun.

Wallace turned to leave, "There is just one thing, boys. Marshal Johnson will let you alone after he gets all your stock and money. He is not apt to molest a poor man." Wallace scratched his face and looked at his right arm, "Yes, the infernal rascal has forged many a warrant to make a few dimes. There is a bunch of ranchers that keep him close to their coattails." Wallace nodded at the boys and walked out to the stairs. The boys did not continue their meals; they were still puzzled by the counsel the sheriff offered. Maybe they finally had a friend in Graham.

"Mr. Denson?" Martha Jane queried. She had driven the fifteen miles out to the settlement of Finis, southwest of Graham. Sheriff Wallace's wife had been so kind as to provide a letter of introduction and a voucher from the sheriff. The man looked up from his work, which seemed to involve staring at a broken plow blade as though the break could somehow cure itself. Over her life, she had noticed that men with no natural mechanical ability would stare at a problem or breakdown like such. Oscar G. Denson finally looked up.

"Yes." He was uncovered and had exposed gallowses that seemed to bother him not, though they embarrassed Martha Jane for him just a bit. "What can I do for you, ma'am?"

"I understand you have some work to be done in exchange for lodging and an interest in the harvest?" Denson nodded and reached up to help her out of the seat. Once inside, she explained her family's situation, and O. G. Denson agreed to help.

CHAPTER 8

JEFFERY'S SALOON
GRAHAM, TEXAS

*J*effery's, as was the custom, was full of the drunk and the almost-there, but Johnson had not paid any attention. He had been waiting outside the back room for a half-hour. He knew that the barons would want to know why the Marlows were out of jail. The brothers had been released one by one as their mother made bail over the past weeks. Most of the barons had been tending their cow hunts and were out of town during the court proceedings, and Johnson did not know what to do. He had hoped the barons would not hear or maybe would not care once they got back into town, or that they might be killed by rustlers or storms. He reminded himself to be delicate when he blamed Wallace for everything. The door opened just a crack, which was his signal to enter. He made sure to take off his John B. when he went in the room. The barons were not standing on formalities, and he was questioned as soon as the door closed.

"So . . . these men who have wronged us are now free." The man who spoke was still dressed for the trail and had kept his hooks and leggings on. He had not shaved in weeks, and Johnson was not sure which baron he was.

"Well, not exactly free. On bail, and they have an arraignment in three weeks, just after the first of the year," Johnson replied.

"Too thin. If these men are the desperados you say, what is to keep them from jumping bail and disappearing?" another of the cattlemen replied.

Johnson coughed and looked at his feet. He was never willing to stand blame for something he could fix on somebody else. "It was their lawyer that done it. Even helped them sell some of their property."

Harmonson was seated by the bar and was still not allowed at the table, not just yet anyway. He had remained quiet up to this point and did not seem to be listening at all. He had a great bowl in front of him that he continuously fed himself from. He would longingly stir his spoon, deliberately rounding up as a large morsel as practicable onto the utensil, then hurriedly stuff it into his mouth, at which time the slow, deliberate pattern returned while he chewed, staring back into the bowl looking for the next potential gob. Johnson would not have guessed he was even listening.

"What can you tell us about that, Arnold?" Harmonson asked the Marlows' mouthpiece in between heapings. Arnold was standing in the far back of the room where etiquette forced him. He had not yet earned even the right of space at the bar.

"I did not make it easy on them. They liquidated all their assets. The judge set an unusually low bail and they met it."

"And did the judge force you to help them find employment as well, or was that you own idea?" Harmonson asked with his mouth full.

"No. Mr. Denson, er, um, also a member of the, um, association was their bondsman and is now their employer. The old woman is tough and bright. She is wise to many things and untrusting where her sons are concerned."

"Oscar Denson?" One of the barons asked Arnold. It was the same one who usually spoke to Johnson. The same one who had threatened to take off his other arm.

"Yes. He owns some property along the Brazos, toward Finis."

"I know where he lives. I do not understand why an association member is assisting these vagabonds," another baron said.

"Well, I am glad we have the confidence of these men who have been stealing from us." He looked at Johnson, "Marshal, what have you learned about the murder capias on the youngest brother?"

"I have telegraphed the sheriff in Vernon. He knew of no papers. Apparently the cowboy Boone killed was not too popular."

All the barons looked up at him, and Harmonson even quit eating. Arnold sensed the heat was off him, and Johnson could feel his relief. The baron who had threatened Johnson got up and walked over, not quickly but deliberately, which forced the marshal to back up to where he could feel the door. Again he put his arm on his shoulder and pulled him as they walked back to the table.

"Marshal, things can get confusing out here. I really want to thank you for your consideration of duty in this case. You have served us well. Sometimes, however, we need to rationalize just a bit. Here, have a seat." Johnson had never been allowed even a few feet inside before, and here he was being offered a seat at the table with the bosses. He noticed Harmonson eyeing him. The baron pulled a chair and sat next to him and continued eating his steak. "Do you have a dog, Marshal?"

"Yes, sir."

"Do you like him?"

"Yes, sir."

"Good." He laughed and looked at his comrades, who joined him. "I would not trust a man who did not like dogs. What does your dog do to its fleas?"

Ed Johnson was completely confused but answered, "Scratch 'em off, I suppose. Kill them."

The baron was pleased, "Right. See, boys, I told you he was smart," the baron said to the others, which caused Johnson to sit a little higher. He had no idea what was going on, but he thought he must be doing something correct. Harmonson was lost in his food again. "Kill them, yes. You see, Marshal, fleas are like nesters. They find someplace that they have no right to and suck the internals out of it. If you don't do something pretty soon, they reproduce, and before long, open property is overcome with them. So sometimes a few suckling nesters have to go down for the property to be of value for the investors, those with risk, who provide back to the community. And sometimes if the men with property appear to let one little thing slide, well . . . it all can be gone. And if we stand by and don't make an example of people accused of stealing horses, well, others will try. Fleas, Marshal, fleas"

The baron cut into his beefsteak. Johnson noticed that he kept his fork in his left hand rather than switching as he himself did, or rather as he used to when he had both arms. The baron swallowed and began again. "All great nations have had great prices to pay. Like the war we just got through with the North, or the Comanche. We lost one and we won one. The Comanche were like nesters, children really, who could never appreciate the value of what they had. Who ever saw a Comanche railroad or bank?" All the barons laughed, and Johnson smiled a little. Harmonson kept eating. "And now the Indian is gone. We still have the Yankees, but perdition, at least they have cash money that spends just right as long as it is spent down here." The other barons knuckle-rolled across the table to show their endorsement. The boss baron put his flatware down and looked hard at Johnson. "And the most important thing is, we are all stronger for the struggle. Do you understand what I've just explained to you?"

"Yes, sir," Johnson lied.

"Good. I knew you were the right man for us. Now, get a capias on the nester trash and get the whole clan back in the jail. We want to be legal with all this. *Sabe?*"

"Yes, sir."

"Thank you, Marshal. I am glad you stopped in for this little chat. Good day to you." And the barons went back to eating their supper. Johnson looked around, nodded at them, and walked out the door.

Johnson gingerly shut the door and walked into the saloon proper. It was fuller now, as most of the local men had eaten their suppers and come into town for entertainment. The tables were all full and the bar was well lined. Most of the local men Johnson knew by name; he also realized they knew what he was doing in the back room. He wanted a drink himself to ward off the chill, then noticed Sheriff Wallace at the far end of the bar. He seemed well into his cups. Johnson put his Stetson back on his head and walked past the bar.

"Why don't you let them boys alone? Or are the barons paying you too much for it?" Wallace said to Johnson as he walked past, loud enough for most of the saloon to hear. Tom Collier was with him. Wallace was grinning the way he always did, as if he was the only one in the place who knew the punch line to a joke. Collier turned his back to the bar and leaned an elbow on it, sipping his draft, wanting to see how Johnson handled the situation. Johnson kept walking, determined not to let Wallace raise his ire. "I will not waste words on a drunkard."

Wallace would not be refused his goof. "So, tell us how you will bring all five boys in with a left-handed gun arm."

Johnson stopped and unconsciously scratched the nub of his right arm. "I can hit a dime on a tree at twenty paces three times out of four, you jackass," he said.

Wallace feigned fear. "Well, boys," he said to the crowd at the bar, "We had all better beware of the southpaw *pistolero.*" The crowd laughed, but Wallace did not join them, only grinned and took another pull on his glass, eyeing Johnson over the lip. Johnson took it as daring him. "Who will place a wager that Johnson can allow three out of four shots fired hit a dime?" Wallace roared loud enough for the saloon's customers to hear. Dozens of men began placing bets as the keep broke out his writing instruments to record. Wallace did not move, just kept sipping and looking at Johnson.

The crowd moved outside into the square with Wallace in the lead, holding a dime up in the air. He found a live-oak and placed the coin between the bark ridges about five feet above the ground and began to exaggerate large steps with the crowd joining his counting, "One, two, three..." all the way to twenty. At twenty Johnson met him.

"I never agreed to height of the target—put it on the trunk," Johnson said.

"The trunk?" Wallace roared. "A man with no arms could throw a rock and hit it three out of four from twenty paces. The dime stays put." The crowd seemed to be agreeing with Wallace. The saloon had emptied, and all were gathered around. Johnson noticed that the barons had left their back room and were standing just inside the bar, watching him through the door, like it was a test of some sort. A brighter man could have guessed they had arranged it all, but Johnson was never accused of overt intelligence.

Johnson shrugged off the crowd and moved to the tree to adjust the dime to his liking.

"Do not touch that dime, lefty," Wallace offered with his hand on his gun. "A bet is a bet." Before Wallace had finished the statement, Johnson had spun around facing Wallace and had drawn and cocked his pistol, aiming it at him. Wallace did not move. Collier stepped in.

"Why, Ed. Marion did not mean nothing by it, he is just funning, you know how he is."

"Shut up, Tom," Wallace said. "Let the cripple shoot me down on the street if he has the nerve. All he does is talk." Wallace had not shown any change in emotion after the draw and kept the grin and his hand on his grip.

"I will show you who is talk." Johnson turned about and took the dime from its nest and placed it on the roots. He then stepped off the twenty paces and aligned himself with Wallace.

"I will show you who is talk," he said again. With that, Johnson drew and fired three out of four shots into the dime, which darted up in the air and around the trunk with each hit. The assembled applauded, and the wagers were paid. Several of the men wanted a double or nothing, and many came over to pat Johnson on the good arm.

Johnson did not acknowledge them or the shooting. He calmly re-loaded his Colt's and continued to stare at Wallace, whose expression remained the same as it had since the incident began. Johnson holstered hard, fixed his hat, and walked across the square to his office, leaving Wallace to do the same.

CHAPTER 9

SHERIFF'S OFFICE
GRAHAM, TEXAS

*M*arshal Ed Johnson tethered his horse outside Sheriff Wallace's office. His first inclination before entering, after the long ride from Vernon, was to dust himself off. Then he remembered whose office it was and muttered, "The devil with him." He stepped in and walked the hallway to the main office, carrying a roll of papers bound in a valise and tied with a thong.

Wallace had his glasses over his carbuncled nose and was leaned back in his catalog-purchased swivel chair with his feet propped up on the desk, a stack of papers on his lap. Johnson did not wait to be acknowledged and tossed the rolled-up paper onto Wallace's lap, startling him and almost causing him to lose his balance. Wallace gained control of the papers, adjusted his spectacles, and looked up.

"Nice to see you, Ed. How is the arm?" Wallace said.

"You drunk, read that if you are able," Johnson replied, indicating the papers he had just tossed. Wallace grinned again, sat up, and pushed the glasses down to the tip of his nose. He began reading the capias. Johnson did not wait and began pacing the office, reciting the speech he had rehearsed all the way from Wilbarger County.

"Boone Marlow is a murderer. A horse thief and a murderer," Johnson said. Wallace thought to interrupt to tell him he said murderer twice, but changed his mind and let Johnson continue.

"That is a capias, legal papers, on a suspect residing under your jurisdiction. You must go and arrest him."

"I cannot help but notice, Ed, there is no reward on the boy. Is that why you are so concerned with my duties rather than going out to Finis and arresting him yourself?"

"Here! There is a fugitive murderer loose in your county. You will go and arrest him, or I will report to the paper your dereliction." Wallace did not answer, only sighed. He genuinely liked the boys and did not care to arrest them.

"Joe!" Wallace shouted. There was no answer, and Leavell, the turnkey, stuck his head around the jamb of the door.

"Go find Tom." Again Leavell did not answer, just moved back into his room. Johnson thought him disobedient until he heard the back door close. Johnson thought, *They think I am bad, here they have a drunk sheriff, a loon for a jailor, and a turncoat deputy.* Collier had been nosing around with Harmonson for weeks, and Johnson knew it. Johnson, convinced he had done his duty, retired from the office.

By the time Collier found Wallace, he was well into his fifth round at Jeffery's. He had gone over as soon as he was sure Johnson was off the square. Collier eventually joined him for a few, then a few more. He was pretty sure the barons would indulge him a few drinks against the December chill, conducting their business. Collier had watched Johnson and, like most, recognized him for the idiot he was. Collier had started talking with Harmonson and P. A. Martin and had finally gained admittance to the back room.

The men in the back room were not the Yankee absentee landowners of the Panhandle and northern plains. They were hard men with harder rules and cash, always cash. They were in a struggle to control the grass, and anything that interfered must be dealt with quickly and harshly. His duty was simple: Safeguard their business interests. If he did well, then he would be safeguarded too. Collier took that to mean financially, and that maybe he would even become the sheriff too. It would be easy enough to keep Wallace distracted and not too much more effort to ruin him.

Collier held back some and let Wallace continue drinking, even encouraging him and buying him a round. They were going to ride out to Finis. Wallace would be too drunk to manage, and Collier would bust this gang. The barons would be grateful. He would clean up the mess Johnson had created too. This evening was sure to propel him in front of the town and the back room. While Collier was imagining his well-earned congratulations from all, Wallace continued talking, mostly about "the bastards in the back room," as he preferred to call them. As much a drunk as he was and considering how much he knew about the barons' operations, it was amazing to Collier that he was still alive, much less sheriff.

Wallace continued talking, and Collier continued nodding, feigning agreement, even throwing in a "Hell, yes," from time to time. Wallace was usually even tempered, but the incident with Johnson over the dime had unnerved him a bit. Wallace was now counting on his fingers, holding his drink in his off hand. "Johnson is also corrupt, incompetent, and in bed with the barons." Wallace tossed back the remainder of his tumbler. His voice was slurred, which proved to Collier that the time was near. He had never seen him so drunk as to not act the opposite. Collier nodded his concurrence and glanced at the back room. Wallace noticed the look.

"Oh, do not worry about them hearing me, Tom. They have all gone to bed with their wives and children. Probably sitting at home by a fire reading the Monkey Ward catalog to their little yard apes, asking what they want for Christmas." Wallace's drink had been refilled. He threw it back and hammered the glass down on the bar to punctuate the statement. The keep filled it up again, glad to have any peace officers in the building, regardless of sobriety. Of course, anyone stupid enough to try mischief in the barons' headquarters would be lynched before they got wet in the Brazos. Collier had to admit, even drunk, Wallace was probably right about the catalog, but guessed he was wrong about their knowledge. The barons' game always kept on and only they knew the rules.

"Well, Tom. It is time to go arrest an innocent boy. Or if he did kill whoever it was up to Vernon, it was probably somebody who deserved killing." Wallace's insides must have convinced him that he had injected enough busthead to keep warm for the thirty-mile trip out and back to Finis. Wallace drank the last shot and placed three dollars on the bar. Without another word, he walked toward, then out, the door. Collier put on his mackinaw and started behind him. He stole one last glance toward the back room. The door was closed, but they still might be in there. They always seemed to know what was going on . . . they were always keen. He nodded at the bartender and walked out behind Wallace.

The norther's wind caught him as soon as he stepped outside. Even the two or three drinks he had did not seem to help. The sky was gray and overcast with winter, which was good. If the clouds held, the temperature would almost be tolerable for the ride back into Graham. Wallace had already mounted and was heading out the Jacksboro road, then to the Finis cutoff. It was past noon and it would be close to nightfall when they arrived. Collier untied his horse, checked the girth, mounted, and trotted out after the sheriff.

Wallace sang most of the way, and Collier joined him on the songs that he knew. Then Wallace would remember why they were out in the weather and become depressed. He liked Boone and the whole family and believed them innocent of the crime. He recalled to Collier that he was not sure how but was convinced the barons were behind that capias. The killing was several years old, and he knew that Johnson had been pleading with the Wilbarger County sheriff for legal paper on the incident for two months or more. Then he just turns up with it one day. As if it had been lost somewhere in the great Wilbarger County's Hall of Justice. Then his mind would feel the warmth again and he would begin singing once more. Collier briefly questioned his own intake of liquor, then rationalized the cold. The amount was just right.

Collier had guessed the arrival closely. It was just dusk when they arrived on the one street in Finis. The whole town was closed and dark with the norther. The town was not really a town at all; just a few buildings and a post office that dutied as a school, and Finis did not even have a lodge yet. The few homes belonged to those who tried desperately to make a living on the Long Bend of the Brazos. But the bluffs were high and the grass poor. Few families stayed more than a season or two. The two lawmen rode down the street to the Marlows' rented, plank, weatherboard cabin.

They reined up at the lone hitching post beside the shack's chimney. As they dismounted, Wallace yelled out, "Halloo, halloo." Collier was surprised at Wallace's lack of caution and stuffed his lead into the sheriff's hands. Wallace began tying both horses and started singing again, while Collier ran over to the porch. For the first time he felt nervous about this. No, he was not nervous; he was afraid. Even in the cold he wiped his sweaty palms on his trousers and swallowed hard. Then he walked as calmly as he knew how over to the door. Tom Collier's time had arrived, and he was not going to let his own fears talk him out of it. Before he could reach the door handle, someone from the inside opened it. It was Elly Marlow, who seemed surprised, though not displeased to see him. The room was crowded with an old plank table and chairs, a bed, several valises, and trunks, weapons, quirts, and other tools of the trail. All of the Marlow clan was in there as well, and they all stopped their activities and stared at the deputy. Collier could feel himself sweating. He knew the Marlows, with their desperate ways, could sense his fear.

"Hello, Tom, light and come in and eat some dinner," Elly said and even extended his hand to Collier. The deputy made no reply to Elly and remained in the doorway.

"It is mealtime here, come on in," someone else said. Collier was not sure who spoke or if he even heard right. There was little doubt that Marlow treachery was laying a trap for him, and he would have to be diligent to escape with his life. He felt the warmness of the liquor again and heard himself speaking.

"I am not hungry." Now was his moment, he felt it just like he was sure all the great men of the plains had when their arrival beckoned. His eyes met Boone's. "Boone, I have come for you." And with that, Collier jerked his revolver and leveled it at Boone. Boone stood up, and Collier felt himself firing the gun directly into Boone's midsection. Instead of seeing the bullet tear into the Marlow, he felt his hand hit by Elly and saw the bullet go splintering into the table, causing Mother Marlow to scream and all the brothers to rise.

Instead of cocking his gun for a second shot, he watched as Boone moved for a yellow boy leaned against the bed near the table. Watched again as Boone chambered a round and leveled it directly at him. It was like he was watching all this happen to someone else, and he could tell that Boone was yelling something at him. When Collier saw Boone's trigger finger twitch, he flinched and heard a loud noise, then felt something burning his left eye socket and temple. It burned real bad, like someone had run a clothes iron hot off the stove onto his face. He felt liquid on that side, but the fluid did not stem the burn any. Then Collier came back from wherever his mind was, and preservation took him over. He slammed the door behind him and ran across the yard into the dark and safety.

Boone chambered another round as the brothers grabbed up their heaters as well. Mother Marlow felt a little bit of life go out of her. She had worked all these months to gain her sons' freedom, and it had all come down to this. She kneeled down where she had sat and began quoting Psalms. Perhaps a few that King David wrote when he was afraid.

Boone stepped out on the front porch and saw a hand holding a pistol in the dark coming around from the chimney end of the building. He took aim and waited a spilt second until the full shape appeared on the porch. When it did, he fired a round into the man's torso. The figure immediately collapsed, lay on the wood, and let out a small groan. Boone caught himself before he allowed a smile and walked over to the intruder.

As soon as he got closer, he realized the man was not Deputy Collier, but Sheriff Wallace. The only person during this affair who had been decent to his family. All the brothers were on the porch now, and they rushed to Boone's side when they heard him cry out. Mother Marlow put aside her reading and joined them on the porch. Boone was cradling Wallace's head in his lap with the yellow boy laid beside him. Boone was crying and telling Wallace he was sorry and that they were going to get him a doctor. Wallace appeared confused; his head flopped around in Boone's lap like a newborn's. There was a dark puddle forming underneath his back as well. Martha Jane realized she did not know what was happening, only that her son had just mortally wounded a peace officer.

"Do not just stand there, you boys get him inside where it is warm. George, put some extra blankets on the floor and make a pallet. Alf, run go find Mr. Denson, tell him what happened and ask his wife to make a poultice, quickly, boy." Alf nodded and took off in the dark. "Elly, better you go to Graham and fetch us a doctor," she said.

With all the activity, they had forgotten about Collier. Wallace was moved onto the pallet and Martha Jane did her best at keeping him calm, though she smelled the drink and assumed that might be helping as much as her words. Perhaps he thought it all a bad dream. So far he had not recognized anyone or said anything intelligible. Boone slammed his hand down on the plankboard table, grabbed his rifle, and walked outside.

"Collier!" Boone yelled.

"What do you want?" Collier's voice cracked from the dark. He had not run far, only to the woodpile near the chimney on the south side of the shack, just outside the light. His voice betrayed his fear and sounded like he had been crying. Charley joined his brother on the porch. "Throw out your gun and come out of the darkness!" Charley yelled. They both heard the thump as Collier's revolver hit the dirt a few feet from the porch. Charley stepped off the porch and grabbed the gun. "All right, come out yourself!" he yelled again. With that, Tom

Collier stepped out, holding his hands up in the air. As he came closer into the light, the brothers detected the snot running and watery eyes. Boone leveled the rifle at his head; Collier was only a few feet away. "Damn you, Tom Collier, you fired on me like I was a dog," Boone said.

"I know, but let us not say anything more about it," Collier sniffed.

Boone kept the '66 leveled at the deputy. "I would not have shot Wallace for the world. Charley, I want to shoot Collier between the eyes—he is the cause of this." With that comment, Tom Collier pissed himself and began sobbing again.

"Boone, put the gun down," Charley said. Collier started walking away toward his horse, and both watched him mount up and leave for Graham.

Denson arrived on the porch out of breath from the run over, followed by his wife and Alf. Outside, the boys heard Denson say, "Oh, my God," when he realized who had been shot. Wallace lay on his pallet and had begun to regain his senses, such as they were. Denson and his wife worked to stem the bleeding, and Martha Jane recounted to Denson as best she could what happened. Wallace said his feet and legs were hurting him and asked her to rub them, which she did, and he blessed her for it. After she made him to understand the events, he came to a little more.

"Sheriff, who shot you?" Denson asked.

"Boone. Tom was justified for what he done," Wallace wheezed. "If you will look in my coat pocket, you will find a capias for Boone." Denson left Wallace and went to his frock, thrown over the back of one of the chairs, in their haste to get at the wound. Inside the right breast pocket he found a large bundle of papers tied with string several times around it. He untied the document and after reading it handed it over to George, who motioned to give it instead to Martha Jane. Martha Jane took the capias and grabbed a lamp, holding it just in between her and the document. She finished reading and returned the document to Denson.

Charles had returned indoors, but Boone remained on the porch. He sat on an upended crate the family used for a stool and kept staring at the puddle of barely visible dark fluid on the wood and remembered that cowboy in Vernon. The shock had worn off, and here he was left with more blood on his hands and more damage done to his family. He began to cry, loudly like when he was a child. He threw the Winchester he had been cradling in his arms onto the porch, away from him, and tried to control the sobs but couldn't. Just then there was his mother, holding his head against her chest, hushing him and soothing him. That made him cry all the harder. He waited for her to tell him it would be all right, but she never did, just kept holding his head and shushing. She separated from Boone and held his face in her hands, forcing him to look at her.

"Now, baby, you have got to put this past you, swallow it down. You will have to ride away from this place tonight and ride hard. Do you remember the night you rode after killing that man at your sister's?" Boone nodded through the tears. Why wasn't she telling him it was going to be all right? "Son, that is exactly what you must do tonight. As soon as Elly gets to town, the laws will come, and with vengeful hearts. They will try to kill you, Boone. You must leave this place of death, and you must do it now. Do you understand, Boone?" Boone nodded again, sniffling, trying to control the situation as best he could. "Good baby." And his mother kissed his forehead. "I will make some victuals for you, and your brothers will pack and saddle the horse. You just stay out here until you get your wits back. No sense those strangers seeing you like this." And Boone was alone again, just like it seemed he always was.

The family was gathered on the porch watching Boone make the final tack adjustments to his horse. He regirthed the saddle, believing it bad luck to let someone else, even a brother, tighten your cinch—like putting a hat on a bed or handing a closed-bladed knife to someone.

The brothers stood silent and their heads were down. George had his hands in his pockets and kicked at a little dust with his boot toe. Boone seemed to be wasting too much time to suit Martha Jane, who stood on the porch holding her Bible.

"Boone, it is time," his mother said.

Boone looked up from the horse's hoof he was examining for the second time. "Yes, ma'am." He put the hoof down and walked past his family into the cabin. Mrs. Denson had Wallace's head cradled in her lap, while Mr. Denson adjusted the abdominal they had made out of an old quilt. The bleeding seemed to have slowed if not stopped, and Wallace did little except stare at the ceiling and blow crimson bubbles out of his nose. Boone walked over and knelt beside him and patted his hair. He knew that he had killed again, not only from the wound's location but the lightless look in the sheriff's eyes. The only man who had been decent to them in Graham. Boone spoke.

"Sheriff?" Wallace continued staring and did not turn his head toward the voice.

"Sheriff? It is me, Boone Marlow." With that, Wallace turned his head and seemed to smile and recognize Boone.

"Why, Boone, it is good to see you again. How is your brothers and ma?"

"They are fine," Boone choked. "I just wanted you to know that I am sorry. I was shooting at Collier, who first shot at me. I did not know you were even on the premises, or so help me I would have held my aim. I would not have shot any man only for good reasons except in self-defense." Tears were rolling down Boone's face, and Denson wanted to shoo him back outside but felt the sheriff was dead anyway and it was Boone who needed the healing.

"So, you thought I was Tom?" Wallace squeezed.

"I certainly did. For God knows I never would have fired, for I have nothing against you," Boone finished. Wallace turned to look at Boone more fully, smiled, and nodded, and then looked back up at the ceiling. Denson eyed Boone, and he saw that the moment was over.

Boone got up and dried his eyes. His family had crowded into the doorway to watch. His mother wiped a tear, the first she had let outside her body since the evening began. Boone looked around in inventory one last time and headed for the door. On the porch he said his goodbyes and received their best wishes. He stepped off the porch and into the stirrup. Once mounted, he turned the horse toward his family on the porch. The tears were all gone and he spoke earnestly.

"In case I am killed while resisting arrest—and I do not intend to be arrested and returned to the Graham jail where I have been mistreated—I do not want any of you to try and avenge me. I shot Wallace and I am willing to pay the penalty, although it was a pure accident— I was aiming to put an end to Collier's cowardly career." With that, Boone turned the horse toward the road and trotted out from the cabin's glow. One of the brothers coughed, and Martha Jane wiped at another tear that managed to escape.

CHAPTER 10

Elly Marlow did not know why he should ride over to the jail. Every instinct he had screamed at him to stay away. But he could not find the sheriff's house and thought the turnkey might be able to help. Wallace's wife must be told about her husband. As far as he knew, Collier had ridden the other direction out of the county. He had already ridden to two different doctors and helped both of them get tacked. Now his horse was well lathered and he was feeling the cold, not having stopped for a blanket coat in all the confusion. It seemed the jail was the only place he knew to go.

He tethered to the rail and beat on the door. Leavell would be in back and it would take him a few minutes to answer. Elly Marlow was never more wrong in his life, and he felt the double-barrel greener in the small of his back. Instinctively his hands went up, well away from the sidearm he was not wearing. He knew it was Leavell and that news had already spread through Graham.

"Go ahead and push on the door. It is open and you are going back to your cell." Leavell said behind him.

"I have done nothing wrong and will not be put back in jail. I only came to town for a doctor and to let Wallace's pards know he has been shot." Elly protested.

"Yes, and one of the doctors has already been here to inform me of your gang's desperate ways tonight. The devil with you and your kin. Go in there, and we will mob the rest." And Leavell kicked Elly though the door.

Tom Collier was still crying when he rode the back way into Graham down Elm Street. He had cleared the story up in his head more. The sheriff had hallooed for all to come out with their hands up, and Boone stepped unto the porch, fired on Collier, then gutshot the sheriff. Collier still had not figured out how he had eventually got the drop on the gang but knew the citizens would believe anything that he told them, especially concerning the popular sheriff.

He heard a conveyance coming quickly from the far side of the square, and Collier pulled his mount into the shadows of the oaks next to the county courthouse. When the vehicle went by, he noticed it was Mrs. Wallace, with a blanket on her lap against the cold and still somewhat in her nightclothes. The buggy was driven by Dr. Price and was soon speeding past him and onto the Jacksboro road toward Finis. Collier thought he heard the doctor calming Mrs. Wallace, saying that it was too soon to worry and that the sheriff was probably just a bit injured and would be fine.

Collier thought about Jeffery's, then thought better. He would need his wits before he went near there. As he came on down Elm and made the turn onto Fourth, there was a crowd already assembled at the jail. Most of the men were on foot, but some were mounted and all were dressed in an assortment of clothing that belied the late nature of the business at hand.

Leavell was on the stoop, holding an axe handle and trying to look like he was in charge. As Collier rounded the corner, one of the mob yelled and they all rushed upon him. The movement was so quick, his horse shied and crow-hopped. This seemed to back the crowd off a bit and let Collier get hold of the horse and his thoughts. They all threw questions at him. What had happened? Was Wallace dead? Where was the rest of the gang? Was he needing a posse? Tom ignored all the inquiries and pushed his horse past the gathered mob and up to the hitching rail. He stepped down, tied his horse, and walked past Leavell into the office. As he closed the door, he heard Leavell outside doing his best to make the mob go home, but they would not have it. He felt the warmth of the building. It was the first time he had felt anything warm in hours. He tried to shut the noise out of his head and fix his mind. When he came into the office, Frank Harmonson greeted him.

"Good evening, Deputy. Had a rough night?" Harmonson was fully dressed and smoking a cigar. He was seated in Wallace's catalog chair and appeared comfortable. Collier paused for a moment and crossed the room, continuing to pull off various garments.

"You might say that," Collier responded. As dependent as he might be on the barons, he had little use for their lapdog tonight. He stopped next to the stove, sat down, and pulled his boots.

Harmonson flicked an ash off the cigar. "You know your turnkey might be doing you more harm than good right now."

"What do you mean? He is trying to dispel a mob. It is the same thing Wallace would have done."

Harmonson rolled the cigar in his hands and blinked. "Wallace is dead or soon will be. You should be more concerned about what others wish to happen rather than a dying drunk." Collier stopped rubbing his feet and looked at Harmonson, who continued, "What I mean is a mob can help us if they are properly motivated and conduct our business interests. Besides, it keeps all of us clean and uninvolved." Collier continued to stare, not grasping anything that had happened tonight or anything that the man was talking about. Harmonson realized this. "Not to worry." And he stood up, gathered his hat, and took a long draft on the stogie. He pointed his hat at Collier, "You tend to your wound and be ready."

"Ready for what?" Collier inquired.

Harmonson adjusted his hat in the small mirror next to the sheriff's desk. He looked at Collier through the reflection at the deputy and smiled. "You just be ready." And he walked to the door and out the back, where there were no witnesses gathered.

And upstairs, above the outside noise, Elly Marlow was straining to listen.

Boone had almost fallen into the Brazos three times. He was cold and the sun would be up soon. Normally a good thing, but not this time. He forced the horse to feel its way along the bluff above the river. He had no plan and did not know where to go. If he stayed along the river or anywhere in the connecting counties, he was a dead man. His horse stumbled again, showing his fatigue. He had ridden hard for several hours, first away from Graham and then back down closer to Finis, hoping to throw off the trail.

After a while they entered the marshy cane breaks, and Boone knew he was near Finis. He also knew that if he did not come up with a plan soon, the laws would find him and probably lynch him on the spot. He knew that the safest place would be the territories. To get to the Red, he would have to cross more country and at night, difficult in even the best situation and impossible with men hunting you and enjoying it. In his desperation, Boone remembered the Indians his family had worked for and his own namesake, Daniel Boone.

He rode until he found some dry ground, at least drier than he had been on all night. As soon as he found it, on a slight bluff, he steadied his horse and began lifting up his legs and taking off his boots and socks. Then he pulled a string off the saddle and tied them together by the pulls, pulled his yellow boy and slid softly down off the horse. He cut the reins so the horse could not step through them and slipped the boots over his shoulder with one boot on either side. He walked Indian style and led the horse back down into the brakes, but before the ground became soft again. Once done, he lifted his hat up in the air and tried to spook the horse away. But the Marlows would never have a head-shy horse, and all the animal did was jerk its head a bit. Boone thought of shooting, then dismissed the thought as stupid. He tried to walk off, but the horse followed. Boone became so upset that the tears almost came again. He would have to hurt the animal. He grabbed his boots and began flinging them on the animal's neck in frustration. He did not realize all the yelling and swearing he had done until the horse finally took off along the cane away from Finis.

Boone felt bad; still, he knew it was better than feeling shot. The horse would be found and returned to Finis. And Denson had seen him ride out on it, so when it turned up alone, he could vouch that the animal was the one Boone Marlow left town on. Boone had also left some of his traps with his name sewn onto the valise.

He knew that the laws and more would soon come. As he made his way barefooted, walking toe to heel so as not to leave a trail a white man could find, he came upon the break in the tree line on the Finis road, across from the town and their cabin. All seemed quiet to him, though there was a buggy he did not recognize outside the cabin. It was just twilight as he made his way into town, ducking between the well-spaced buildings. If he hid in a building they would find him as sure as if he went back into the cabin or to Denson's. Corn cribs and lofts were out as well.

He stood behind a building and watched his cabin. The door was opened and he saw his brothers, Denson, and another man carry

Wallace to the buggy. There was a woman whom he did not recognize, who might have been crying a bit. He did not see his mother and presumed she was inside praying. For all the care they gave Wallace, he must have still been alive, and Boone offered a prayer of thanks for that. Maybe the wound was not that bad and the sheriff would recover and clear Boone of the crime. But he knew that gut wounds took a long time to kill. Once they got Wallace inside the vehicle, the man and woman Boone did not know got in and drove away toward Graham. His brothers and Denson stayed on the porch a moment talking. Denson called for his wife, who joined him from inside, and the two walked back to their house. Boone heard George thank them and apologize; Denson did not look back, only waved. The brothers went back inside, where their mother would have them join her in prayer. Boone hoped that with all the praying for the sheriff's mortal life and immortal soul that would go on, his family would remember him as well.

With Finis empty again, Boone saw his only option: a haystack right behind the Marlows' cabin, not two hundred yards away. He listened closely for any sounds and made his way to the stack, crawled in, and began to hollow out a space.

Once comfortable as possible, he pulled off his frock and wrapped it around himself. Slightly warmer as twilight came and went, he said his final prayer of the day and drifted off to sleep.

Denson was having trouble sleeping. Christmas Eve was not going to be much of a holiday for the morrow. Wallace had been in and out of a coma for days. It did not look good. Denson knew from the moment he had arrived at the Marlows' cabin. This was further confirmed by the look on Doc Price's face when he saw the wound. Nevertheless, he had plenty of work to do, and lack of sleep would not help any. He drifted.

He awoke to Frank Harmonson sitting in a chair in his room and looking out the window. Denson sat up straight.

"Evening, O. G." Harmonson pulled his timepiece and corrected himself, "Or rather, morning. Sleeping well?"

Denson did not know what Harmonson was doing here or how he got in. He was glad his wife had begun sleeping in a separate room due to his snoring. Hopefully, she was not a light sleeper this night. Denson did not know how it might end. Harmonson struck a match and lit the lamp beside his chair.

"Odd that a member of the association keeps such interesting company, is it not, O. G.?"

"What do you mean?" Denson tried to hedge. He was a charter member of the association. Had one of the first brands registered in Young County. Denson knew word had gotten out about the bonds and employment. He just didn't know what the barons would do about it. The shooting of Wallace had elevated the situation.

Harmonson smiled. He pulled a cigar, licked his fingertips, then lifted the glass on the lamp. He twirled the cigar over the flame until he got a nice red ring. He had seen the one of the barons do this, and he liked the touch. "Oh, you know exactly what I mean. You bonded those boys out of jail. They would be rotting in Huntsville, or worse, if you had not helped them out. If that was not enough, you gave them employment and a place to live. How nice of you."

Denson swung out of bed. He walked over to the window and opened it, without bothering to put on a robe over his nightshirt. His wife must not smell the smoke; the cold outside did not matter right now. "It was the Christian thing to do, Frank," Denson snapped.

Harmonson took a draft on the cigar, "Christian. How nice."

"At any rate, what do you want me to do about it now?"

"O. G., Wallace will probably die tonight. If not tonight, then to-morrow or the next day. Personally, I think we should give a reward to the Marlows for ridding Young County of the drunk. I would love to sit around and chitchat with you about how glad I will be when Wallace takes his dirt nap, but we know that is not why I am here."

"Why are you here?" Denson sat back down on the bed. The wind was cold through the open window. Denson did not care.

"We have one of them in jail now. As soon as Wallace quits breathing, Collier will need to arrest the remainder of the gang."

"Family," Denson corrected.

"Yes, family. You see, O. G., You can still be helpful to us. Anyway, your associates wish you," Harmonson leaned forward, exhaling the smoke as he said it, "in the strongest way, to cancel your bonds on the rest of the brothers. We do not need any more matters interfering with due process. We, your associates, want this to be legal."

"What if I do not?"

Harmonson smiled and flicked his ash onto the windowsill. He sat back in the chair. "Now, O. G., we do not need to talk about unpleasantness. Do we?" And he kept smiling, looking at the red glow and blowing on it.

Denson covered his bare legs some with the covers and looked down. "No, I guess we do not." Denson knew what he meant. Men who would come in the night. There would be no witnesses. "What about their mother?" Denson asked. He could not turn her out.

"What do I care about the old bitch?" Harmonson flicked another ash out the window and stood up. "You do with her as you think best, O. G. I would not go advertising if I let her stay, however."

Denson nodded. He did not get up or look at Harmonson.

"Do not get up. I can let myself out." Harmonson turned to leave the room. "O. G.?"

"Yes," Denson answered, but kept looking at the floor.

"Close that damned window and get some covers on. You will catch your death." And Harmonson left the room. Denson waited until he heard the front door click before he lay back into his bed. There would be little work done tomorrow.

CHAPTER 11

OAK GROVE CEMETERY
GRAHAM, TEXAS

*W*allace died. He had passed the day before, on Christmas Eve. It was a surprise to all that he had lasted a week with a gut wound. He never came around much, except to ask what time it was and for his bottle. Even with all the laudanum in him, he still craved his hooch. The drug must have been poor succor compared to the bottle. Perhaps in the end, as it always had, drink provided him with security. At least the sheriff had passed warm and in bed, which had always been his great desire. And there was not too much pain; the doctor had given him large amounts of the opiate to overcome his tolerance to intoxicants.

Some had wanted Mrs. Wallace to wait for the day after Christmas to inter her husband, but she refused. The hardware store owner, Morrison, had even spoken with her himself. There were even more embalming supplies due in from Dallas, and he could be properly cared for. She would hear none of it. O. G. Denson stood away from the large crowd at the cemetery while the reverend finished up the eulogy. Once he was through, there was a hymn, though no one much heard the title spoken through the rain and sleet, and everybody kind of hummed what they believed the tune to be. When the verse finished, the Freemasons began their farewell, Denson cursed himself for forgetting his apron, but it was just as well. Several people believed he had played a part in the sheriff's death.

Denson looked at the hole in the ground and noticed there were little waterfalls coming over the lip of the grave on all four sides. Then he thought of another song that folks sang when they were melancholy, and he sang it in his mind for a few bars: *In a narrow grave, just six by three, bury me not on the lone prairie.* And Denson sniffed. It was a sad song.

The few umbrellas were held over the ladies attending, mostly to support the widow Wallace, who was well liked. She had almost passed out during the church service, but seemed to have found some strength since then.

Martha Jane had wanted to attend, to try to repay Mrs. Wallace's kindness to her family, but Denson talked her out of it. Even though all knew Martha Jane to be blameless in the killing, she was the mother of a fugitive wanted for two murders, and Denson convinced her to remain in prayer and at home. He would attend in her stead and present their sorrows to the Wallaces. She spoke of her concern over the sheriff's soul and his drinking. Denson said that would be a fine thing to pray on and convinced her that Wallace was a veteran, and that no man who had faced death on so many battlefields could ever be anything but a Christian. She seemed satisfied and even allowed a little smile.

Denson stole another peek over the wet shoulders of the crowd and noticed that Mrs. Wallace did not seem to know nor care where she was. Her umbrella was tilted over her shoulder, and the rain and sleet mussed her bonnet and what little makeup dignity allowed. No one else seemed to see it, and that made Denson sad. As the well-wishers made their way past her, taking her hand, she seemed limp and kept staring past everybody. She did not seem stoic or strong, merely showed no emotion whatsoever. Denson could not make out what she was so keen on, so he assumed it must be the casket.

There was a rumor that she had been expecting his death for some time. A Tonkawa witch woman, who was living down in the salt flats, had walked up to her on Grove Street and told her that "her man was going to die." Then the witch began a song, and nobody knew what she was singing. Mrs. Wallace, polite as always, blushed and excused herself across the street. Over the next few months, she paid little attention initially, but the omen worried her. Maybe she felt her husband's liver would not last, after all.

Denson broke his promise to Martha Jane and did not pass condolences to Mrs. Wallace. He broke up with the rear of the crowd and made his way toward his buggy, parked just outside the cemetery gate. Stepping gingerly between the markers, he noticed Tom Collier talking to someone in a surrey. Behind the vehicle were ten or so mounted men. All were wearing talmas and fish over their mackinaws and blanket coats. Denson kept walking and stole a glance every few steps to see who it was with Collier.

He eventually saw that it was Harmonson with P. A. Martin. Both had probably stayed outside the grounds, parked on the road. Nice and dry in the vehicle. Denson kept walking and looking; the sleet and rain were too bad for them to notice his looks. Harmonson, as usual, seemed to be giving the orders. All Collier did, with his head leaned in the buggy to keep it dry, was nod. He did not appear to be talking, just nodding his head.

Denson made it to his surrey, stepped in, and released the brake. The horse had fallen asleep. It always amazed Denson that horses could sleep standing up and in any kind of weather. He looked over at Harmonson again. Collier had turned and mounted his horse. Harmonson leaned out into the wet and spoke some more to Collier. The new sheriff nodded again and gave a little wave of his hand, then turned and rode back into Graham. Harmonson finally noticed O. G. and nodded. Marshal Ed Johnson was conspicuously absent from the meeting.

Denson stirred the dray, waking the horse that startled a step or two. He was to drive over to the sheriff's office and cancel his bonds on the brothers. He looked one last time at the graveside and saw the Negroes who tended the cemetery lowering Wallace's casket into the ground. They seemed to be singing, though Denson was unsure.

⊷⊛⊶

The good citizens of Young County had named Tom Collier as sheriff the day after Wallace was shot, and now here he was leading a posse out to Finis to arrest the rest of the Marlow "gang." Some of the men were from Graham, some from the surrounding communities like Belknap. All had been recommended to him by Harmonson. With Elly Marlow still in jail, he was to ride out and arrest the other three brothers as accessories to murder, even had papers to show for it.

All the way out to Finis, he filled his party with stories of how Wallace had been dealt with by the Marlow trash. It was Collier who had prevented them from any further transgressions or damage done to the sheriff. He was glad they all seemed game to listen and not ask too many questions, because he had not told the same story twice yet, but all seemed interested. For some reason, he had come out that night a hero in the town. It was the first time anybody thought Tom Collier a hero, and he was not going to do anything but encourage it.

The sleet abated about the time they arrived in Finis, and the sun peeped out just a bit, though the wind had not stopped at all. The plan was simple; ride up to the cabin, surround it, and halloo for them to come out. Tom would do all the talking and had ordered all the men to bring greeners or coach guns if they had them. As they rode up to the cabin, Collier took his time and motioned for the deputies to position themselves for anything the gang might do. Then he hallooed at the cabin.

It was Charley who stepped out, in shirtsleeves, wiping his hands on a cloth. Collier did not wait for him to speak.

"Charley, Wallace has died, your bondsman has given up, and you will have to go to jail."

"Jail? For what? No one here had anything to do with Wallace's shooting," Charley replied.

"Nevertheless, I have papers, and you and your brothers will collect your traps and accompany me back to jail." Collier could feel all his deputies staring at him, evaluating his performance, like a bull at the auction barn. That was just fine with Collier. He was up for the performance and believed the hero role fit him fine. Collier caught himself smiling as he looked down at Charley. The posse would all be talking in the bars tonight of how Tom Collier brought in the Marlow gang.

Boone had gotten his water from the horse trough at first. He waited until just before dawn, when there would be not alert posse around. It looked to him like every man in Jack and Young counties was after him; they searched every barn and well in Finis near, and they seemed to make a habit of returning to the Marlow cabin every day or so to tear it apart again and again. It got so bad that he considered coming out, but he knew his family did not want that either. After a few days, some men brought his horse back to his mother, and that made Boone happy. This seemed to convince the laws that he was gone for sure.

The very next day at twilight, he saw his mother coming into the field were he lay hidden. All he had drunk was horse water and he had eaten all the victuals his mother had prepared. Another norther had blown in, and the rain and sleet almost made Boone try one of the barns. The haystack protected him some from the wind but none from the wet. When she passed within a few feet, he took one of his cartridges and tossed it at her. Martha Jane heard something hit the ground, and while she looked around her, she heard a muffled, "Mama."

She glanced at the noise, and all she saw was a haystack. Then in the dusk she saw her youngest son's face peering through at her. Her first thought was joy, and she wanted so badly to run to him, take care of him, but she caught herself. She straightened up, looked to see if there were any deputies around, and calmly walked back to the house. Boone immediately frowned. Was she mad at him or did she not see him? He could not tell in the almost dark. Martha Jane did not walk directly back to the house. She kept her general direction, easing herself over to the stack. Boone got excited and started to rush out to her. She got a little closer and said without stopping or looking at him, "Expect you are hungry but healthy. I will run you out some supper in a few hours. Do not leave the stack. They is still deputies around and about." And Martha Jane kept walking. Boone felt himself relax for the first time in a week. He did not even pay attention to his belly stuck to his backside as he slept a little and imagined the feast his mother would soon bring him.

"Boone. Boone, wake up. I cannot stand out here long." It was just after midnight. Boone stuck his face above the hay. It was his mother, holding a mucket and canteen. She knelt and lay them down next to the stack, where Boone could reach them without exposing himself. He glanced around. "Do not worry, we are in the clear just yet. Wait until I am gone a few minutes and then get them. I will be out before sunrise with your breakfast." Boone started to get out, and his mother stopped him. "No need to be reckless. Wait until I am gone. You are on a slight rise of ground, and someone could see your silhouette. They will pay no attention to me." Boone nodded. He was glad to see his mother again. He could smell her, and it was good. "Baby, I have something else to tell you. The sheriff died from your bullet yesterday. They forced Denson to forego his bond on all of you, and they came and arrested your brothers for accessories to murder. I do not know what 'accessories' is, but am sure it is not good." Boone did not reply. He had known instantly that Wallace would not live long; still, he was shocked that his brothers were implicated, that he had implicated them by his actions. It was his fault. Everything he had ever touched or done always went wrong.

"The governor has also put a reward out for you."

Boone choked, "How much?"

"It was two hundred dollars, but now that Wallace has died they have raised it to seventeen hundred dollars, or so the posse said." Boone knew then that his life was over and there would be no place to run, in Texas or the territories. Martha Jane knew this was hurting Boone, her only son not in jail. "Boone, do not do anything stupid. I am fine and have some supplies put back and we have a little money. Stay put until I can figure out what to do with you. I will speak to you again in the morning." And his mother turned and walked back to the cabin. Boone watched her go as far as the starlight let him. Then he reached out, grabbed his mucket, and ate his dinner. And he wondered what the person who collected the seventeen hundred dollars for his life would spend it on.

PART III

CHAPTER 12

ome of the heat that passed from the first floor warmed things up a bit, but not much. The boys had only brought their coats and were not allowed the time to gather any blankets from their cabin. Each cell had one or two moth-eaten jean blankets, nothing to keep the chill away, and there was no stove.

The boys shared the southern cell together because the one other cell, on the north side of the floor, was usually loaded with one or two drunks, transients, or transfers to another district. The brothers were fed separately from the other prisoners, and sometimes not at all.

The Marlow boys were friendly but struck up no friendships with any of their cellmates. There was the occasional nod and greeting but nothing more. No doubt all of the temporary occupants were intimidated by reputation of the "Marlow gang." Sometimes as the brothers arose they would see that new prisoners had been moved in overnight, and they would always be staring in at the sleeping brothers, imagining tales of the James and Youngers.

The Marlows did not seem to mind and were even somewhat flattered by the attention. They did desire privacy and had taken to hanging the sole cell blanket on the bars whenever they wanted to parley amongst themselves. George had heard about laws placing spies in with prisoners to trick them. Elly had told them the night they came in about the mob talk he had heard Collier and someone else discussing on the first floor. Several of the transient prisoners had also told the Marlows that they had heard the same.

The new pair that shared the northern cell were especially interested in the brothers' story. Particularly the one who appeared to be the younger of the two. Every chance he caught one of the brothers' eyes, he began asking questions about shooting a law. It was plain the two had no love of peace officers or their duties, and after a day or so the brothers warmed up a bit. The two were from Arkansas and were being extradited back there for horse stealing. "A good thing it was Arkansas and not Texas, else we would hang for horse thievery as sure as you boys will for your crime," one of the pair offered. The comment was offered in the spirit of respect for the Marlows' deed and with a sense of camaraderie, yet tough talk did not impress the brothers. The Marlows let it pass. They exchanged names, though the brothers could not remember them and began calling them Arkansas Number One and Two. Not because of their age but because of the number of front teeth each one showed.

Arkansas Number Two seemed the most helpful and could see more of the town from his window. He let them know when crowds were outside and who came and went into the jail. He did not know names but gave good enough descriptions to let the boys have an idea. One evening after supper and a long conversation about a mob up in Dodge City, Arkansas Number Two offered an idea.

"I have a knife," he said.

The brothers had put up their obligatory blanket and were busy telling the story to each other when the interruption came. The talk stopped. Arkansas Number One looked at Number Two and spoke again.

"I said I have a knife," he said again and giggled. With that, he saw George's face poke past the corner of the jean. George was in no mood for jokes, which Number Two was sometimes fond of making.

"And what does that mean to my brothers and me?" George responded.

"It means I will give it to you right now, if you want it. No charge either." Arkansas Number One sat on the bunk quiet, watching his confederate negotiate.

"You do not believe me, do you?" And he looked toward the door, reached into his trousers in the back, and pulled a Barlow out. It was not a big weapon, but bigger than any had just now. "It is three bladed and is sharp enough to slit Leavell's throat from ear to ear," Number Two grinned. George did not know what to do or say. Number Two was excited. This was his chance to help out some desperate men. Desperate men always had their stories told, and maybe he would be remembered in those tales and thanked for the big prison break. Just like William Bonney had done in Lincoln County, New Mexico, a few years back.

Number Two walked to the far side of the cage and reached for a broom leaning against the wall. His fingers just closed on it and he pulled it into the cell with him. That done, he pulled the longest blade from the knife, stuck the point into the wooden handle, and passed the broom, knife end first, over to George, who took it immediately.

George pulled the knife out of the stick, and Number Two slid the broom back through his bars, walked to the opposite side, and set the broom back up against the wall as near as he could to its original place. Then he turned and grinned again at George, who was looking at the knife. Number Two swatted Number One on the shoulder; he was beside himself with their pending fame. George looked at the knife, then nodded and smiled back at the Arkansas horse thieves.

The brothers would not kill Leavell. Over the next several days, they took turns at night chipping away at the sandstone wall. Where they had earlier cursed being on the south side away from the street, now they rejoiced in it. During the day they covered the ever-enlarging hole with the lone jean blanket. One time they thought Leavell was on to them when he asked what the blanket was doing hanging on the wall. "Why, we are just letting it air out after the night so the next brother can use it." George replied, which must have satisfied Leavell, because he mentioned it no more. They scooped the sand into the chamber pots, confident the turnkey would not investigate the substance flow too carefully.

Arkansas Number One and Two continued to watch and even stood guard so all the brothers could contribute. For once, luck seemed to be with the brothers as there had been no more late-night prisoners dropped off from the bawdyhouses or area lawmen.

It took only a few days for them to carve through the soft rock, and then there was a man-sized hole through all but the last inch of wall. That part would be kicked out when they made their move.

That afternoon they determined to escape after midnight. Just before the supper meal it began to rain heavily. George said that would be good and would slow down any posse traveling on the roads. They all agreed to go one hour after Collier's final bed check.

It was after midnight and still raining. Collier had not come yet.

Number One and Two took turns at the window. There was no activity on the streets, even at Jeffery's, which could be seen to the west if a person pressed hard against the bars and turned the eyes until they hurt. Charles was for going anyway.

"If we wait any longer, they will find the hole and mob us anyway. We must leave now."

George disagreed, "He is only a little late tonight. If he comes in here a few minutes after we have escaped, they will catch up to us in no time and shoot us down like dogs."

"At least we will have a chance, brother, because that is just what they are going to do anyway. Collier is probably holed up someplace and does not want to come out in the cold and wet. I say we leave now," Charley said. George relented, and with that the brothers took down the blanket and begin tearing it into strips. Elly was quite the rope maker and had fashioned a weave with the jean in a few minutes. The brothers said their goodbyes to Number One and Two, tied the blanket to a bar, kicked out the last inch of sandstone wall, and one by one slid into the wet night.

The rain and Harmonson had held up Tom Collier. Frank had told him that Johnson was upset over the Wallace affair and was not talking with the barons anymore. Had said he did not care if it cost him his life. Johnson would not assist the barons in their skullduggery. That was fine with Harmonson, who figured the one-armed marshal a liability anyway. He had asked Collier if he was interested in the marshal's job once Johnson was gone. Collier had replied that he did not know just yet. Then Harmonson left Jeffery's and Collier followed.

The rain had stopped, but the streets were a quagmire of slop. Somebody had thought to put boards out, and Collier used these as best he could to negotiate the short walk back to the jail. By the time he arrived, his boots were caked in mud. He took off the heavy footwear and opened the door. He walked down the hallway, absorbing the building's heat and thinking how nice his bed would feel in a few minutes. He might even sleep in tomorrow. He still felt odd sleeping in the jail. He had been a boarder at the Wallace boarding house since he took the job but had not been comfortable there since Wallace's death. He stopped at the stairs and considered going on to bed. Surely Leavell had checked the prisoners when he had not shown up. Then he heard the turnkey snoring and remembered who he was thinking about. He climbed the stairs to just make sure.

"What time is it?" George asked again.

"I told you it is nearly 8:00. Ma will have been up for hours. We just have a few more miles to go," Charley answered. The boys had made slow progress in the silky mud but had stayed on the road regardless. They were unsure of the route across country and knew that traveling the river would be worse. The mud had been bad for them, and George knew any posse could follow their trail. He had regretted the decision the moment they hit the ground, but by then it was too late. Now their only chance was to make it to the cabin and then ride fast horses to the territories. Even meet up with Boone if they could find him. Martha Jane would not be pleased, but it was better than having mobbed sons.

They were in a field just off the road and were angling fast toward the next woodline. There was already a farmer in the field surveying for water damage with his son. He looked up and saw the mud-covered group, waved, and went back to his field as if it was an everyday sight to see. Just before they hit the trees, George's heart sank. A line of horsemen, ten or twelve, was waiting on them.

"Throw away your guns, or be killed!" a voice yelled. The brothers all recognized it as Collier's. The brothers stopped. They were too tired and cold to run, and deep inside, the capture came as a relief. At least it was over and they could go back to the warmth. George was not feeling as charitable.

"Shut up!" he shouted back at Collier. "Or I will knock you off your horse with a rock. You know we do not have any guns." Then George stuck his hands in the air and was followed by his brothers. The farmer turned from his work and watched, then once again went back to his survey.

The posse had brought a wagon, and George did not know how that would get them back to Graham with the road poor. The team managed; however, it seemed to take longer than their walk out. Once in town, the wagon passed the jail and went to the livery. It was past noon, and the people on the streets stopped and pointed. George guessed it was the mud covering them, or their infamy, or both that drew the fingers and the gossip.

There was a large crowd outside the Boyles & Gamble Stable and it was standing room only inside. As they got closer, a few people started yelling to get a rope, but George knew it was bravado. He saw no ropes. Bandits with ropes stole you in the night, with no witnesses. The brothers were unloaded, two at a time, and taken inside with Collier and three deputies. The others stayed in the wagon and watched. George and Elly were first.

Inside there was a furnace, and Tom Collier was standing next to it holding a set of leg irons. Collier was smiling and cradling his Henry. He tossed the irons to the smith and looked back at the two brothers. "Now, you murderers, I guess you will not get away again."

CHAPTER 13

MARLOW CABIN
FINIS, TEXAS

*M*artha Jane sat on her bed and combed her hair. It was down, and she fingered the graying locks that had once been dark brown with just a hint of red. About the color of Elly's hair, she remembered. She had said her prayers and would have to get up in a few hours to feed Boone again. She still waited until after midnight, just in case there was someone watching the place. A few nights ago she had moved Boone into the corn crib closer to the house. It had been searched many times, and for weeks no one had looked into there.

She heard footsteps on the porch and thought it might be Denson looking in on her before he went to bed himself. She had been careful not to tell where Boone was or even hint that she was not concerned over his whereabouts. She did not want to mislead Denson. She guessed it was better than him knowing the truth and asking him to mislead others. She was a sinner and would do her best to keep sins to herself without asking others to test God and the authorities.

Now there was a knock on the door, and Martha Jane gathered her dressing gown and put on a shawl. She went to the door and opened it. Standing there were two men she did not recognize. They sported badges, and she could smell the alcohol from where she stood. She took the surprised look from her face and confronted the men.

"The posse has been here several times. There is no one here but myself, and I would think a widow would be allowed some decency in her nightclothes. One of them smiled at her and started to speak, then the other one began instead, his words slurred with drink.

"You may be a widow, but you are also harboring an outlaw. A law-abiding citizen surely would not object to legal officers searching, no matter the time." And he walked in past her. His partner followed. She turned with the door still opened as the men began walking around the small room as if they did not know where to begin. It did not last long. The talker walked over to the bed, and rather than bending down he reached under and flung the entire frame over. His partner joined in. Within minutes the two had demolished the entire room and did not even seem surprised that they did not find Boone. Martha Jane wanted to protect her property but knew she could not stand against these men. If something happened to her there would be no one to look after her sons.

"What is in this?" the talker asked, indicating a large trunk.

Martha Jane stammered, trying to remember what was in it. "It is—*was* my husband's. It contains some of his medical supplies and books. Please leave here, you can see there is nothing here for you."

"Medical supplies, huh? Like laudanum?" And he performed a motion similar to the bed, reached down and unlatched the trunk, motioned to his confederate who grabbed one handle and he the other. Then they lifted it up and dumped its contents on the hardwood floors. Martha Jane was in shock. All of the men who had searched here before had been courteous to a fault and left as quickly as they came, spending most of their time on the property. It was plain that no one could hide well or long in a single-room cabin. The two were laughing now and got down on their knees to rummage through her dead husband's nostrums. All she had to remember him by.

Martha Jane realized that the evening might end more horribly than it had begun. The two were holding up books and vials to the light, trying to pronounce words of which they had no knowledge.

"Whooee. If there is any of that opium in here, I will be tickled," the talker one said, looking at vials and tossing them aside just as quickly. They scattered through purgatives, Seton needles, and one hard rubber enema. There was even a lancet and some scales. There were several books with titles such as *Gunn's New Family Physician: or Home Book of Health* and *The Principles and Practice of Modern Surgery*, but the men did not look at those. Martha Jane knew she must make a move. As the men were occupied, she walked over to the fireplace and grabbed her poke. It contained all she really believed she would ever need, a Testament and a Colt's revolver. She opened the drawstring and pulled the gun quietly from the bag. Neither man was paying her any attention and they kept at their hunt until they heard the gun's half-cock. Both looked up, first at the lady in her nightclothes with her hair down, then at the barrel of the pistol.

"Now, boys, I have asked you to leave and I meant it," Martha Jane said. Neither man moved, except for the talker, whose hand wandered back to his own pistol. Martha Jane caught it.

"You do not know how to shoot that," he offered and stood up and took a step toward her.

"There has been enough death here. But I will be obliged to cause more if you do not leave this house at once."

The man stopped his momentum when she fully cocked the hammer. She added, "God help me, I will end your life if you do not leave this place now." The talker swallowed and nodded. He lifted his hands away from his gun and moved slowly. Martha Jane stepped away from the door and allowed the men the room to walk out, well away from her. The men seemed more embarrassed than afraid, which was fine with her so long as they left. The two never regained eye contact, and she followed them out onto the porch and heard them get mounted and ride into the night. She stayed on the porch a little while to make sure they would not come back. Once satisfied, she went back into the cabin.

After locking the door, she placed the gun back into her poke. She kept out her testament and placed it close to her heart, took off her dressing gown, and sat back on the bed. She searched in the covers for her brush and began combing her hair. Her mother had told her to brush it every night one hundred strokes, and she always had. After the first few brushes, she began to weep just a bit. She tried to stop crying, and was not quite sure why she was doing it. The more she tried to stop, the more the tears came. Finally, she gave in to the anguish and put her face in her hands and let it come. She heard herself sobbing loudly and then noticed a presence in the room. She did not care—let them kill an old woman weeping for herself and her sons. Everything she had ever wanted for her family had been taken away. Things would never be right. Then the presence spoke.

"Mama, are you all right?" Boone said. He had come in the back door, which she had not locked. She did not counsel him for leaving his hideout; she reached up and pulled him down to her. Then she buried her face in his chest and cried and cried. Boone had never seen his mother cry except at his father's funeral, and then only for a bit. She was wailing like a child and clinging to him. This role reversal shocked him, but if it was what his mother needed, then that was that. He let her cry, stroking her hair, and did not say anything at all.

Boone finished putting his traps together. They were laid out on the bed, and he mentally inventoried them two or three time before packing each item. There was a mackinaw, waterproof, cartridges, his '66, and a Testament. Martha Jane watched and knew he had inherited this habit from his father. Doctor Marlow was also thorough with his personal items and like Boone did not allow the habit to intrude on more important matters where it would have been better served.

Satisfied, Boone rolled the final items into his blanket and tied them with two strands of latigo. He walked over and hugged his mother again, not for goodbye—not yet—just for support. He patted her back.

"It is going to be all right, Mama. I will make it fine." Martha Jane pushed him away and pursed her lip. Boone recognized the expression and realized he had said something wrong.

"No! No, you will not." She pushed him again. "You will get on your horse and ride away from here tonight, and this time stay away." Boone looked down, and she knew she had hurt him, but she knew he might be the only one of the brothers to live and she wanted him gone. Boone sat down on the bed and continued staring at the floor.

"Where will I go?" Boone asked, on the verge of crying himself.

"I do not want to know—away from here to be sure." She walked over and kissed the top of his bowed head and squeezed his shoulders. "Now, finish up and go and saddle your horse. I have some money you can take with you." And she walked away from Boone and out to the front porch.

❈

Frank Harmonson let the wild talk continue. His job here at the Belknap Masonic Lodge Number 660 was to instigate, but not necessarily take the lead.

Several bottles were getting passed around, and that was grand. He had seen to it that word spread among the town's property owners and never let on who had called the meeting. When pressed, he would change the subject or imply that perhaps some persons might not be mature enough to deal with the serious matters that were to be discussed, or so he had heard would be discussed. He had been careful not to talk to any clergy or other do-gooders who would inevitably bring up the right to trial and all that garbage. He had let it be known that it was Charley, not Boone, who had killed Wallace. It was a lie, of course, but it served its purpose. The idiots had never found Boone, nor even a trail, and something had to be done to stir them up. Nobody would ever mob prisoners unless there was good reason.

From the fifteen or so gathered, it looked as if he had selected well. If someone from the assembled grabbed on to the leadership, why, that was just fine with Harmonson and his employers. Then all that would need doing was to keep them steered in the right direction. Which was also fine with Harmonson, who took pride in his ability to steer. He believed that "steering" might even be the highest form of leadership known. Ofttimes he thought if he had known Christ he could have shown him the way to true stewardship; always let others do the work. Don't go into the temple yourself. Get the disciples riled up and let them run off the moneychangers. Harmonson quit thinking and listened to his disciples talk.

"They have killed the sheriff and tried to escape once. Will we just let them try again until they succeed and burn the town down?" It was P. A. Martin delivering a well-rehearsed monologue. Practiced all the way to the town of Belknap from Graham while Martin drove Harmonson and his buggy.

Someone responded, "P. A. is correct; Collier says the governor is wrong with the reward for Boone and that it was Charley Marlow that spilt Wallace's blood." Harmonson nodded his agreement. Collier had gotten nervous about Boone's escape and began massaging his recollection from Boone to Charley pulling the trigger. It had been easy, and Collier was a natural at it. Even with Wallace stating it was Boone who shot him, folks believed what they chose to.

Things should progress well now. So far nobody had publicly mentioned mob, and Harmonson had relayed strict orders from the barons that nobody from the back room would mention the word. Let the others do that.

"The Marlows ought to be punished. They ought to be hanged!" another man offered. Hanged was close but not quite there.

"Old lady Marlow has raised her sons to be murderers and horse thieves, and they all ought to be killed," one more said above the growing din. Martin stared nervously at Harmonson, who mouthed *wait* back at him.

"I would tie the rope to hang any one of them." Harmonson

looked for who said it, and Martin gave a shrug when he caught his eyes. That was all the room needed. Somebody had finally tossed the horse apple onto the table, and the mob talk finally began in earnest. "They ought to be mobbed, and I am willing to help at any time!" Soon a complete plan, down to who would provide the ropes and disguises, was finalized, and the mob was happy. The event would occur the next evening. Sometime after the crowd had decided their direction, Harmonson and Martin left the building and headed back to Graham.

CHAPTER 14

*T*here was little left for Tom Collier to do at the jail, and it was almost 9:00 P.M. He gathered up his coat and gloves and made the biggest show he knew how to of leaving for the night. The night before, he had stayed out of town, riding around the county, letting people see him performing the taxpayers' business. He would stop occasionally and visit with folks as he covered the county's municipals from Throckmorton to Olney and back to Graham. He made sure he attended the saloons for just a minute or so. "No," he would say when offered a drink, "I must be back to my duties—there is an outlaw on the loose." Then he would drop a hint or two that it might have been Charley Marlow who killed Wallace. The patrons would nod and become self-righteous about the murder, then make another attempt at drink, and then he would leave. He had remained away from Belknap, where he knew a certain meeting was being held. He had wanted to attend, but Harmonson thought better. "Tom," Harmonson said condescendingly, "leave this work to those mentally prepared to do it." And he had left it at that; Throckmorton, Olney, and then Graham. Just so folks in the county saw him out and about at all hours—that should show anybody who came looking that he was serious in his duties and that he had no connection with the jail on that night.

He had stayed out late with no sleep and been especially diligent and visible during the day, so when he made his excuses to go sleep in his old room at the widow Wallace's house, no one would even consider it a problem. So he continued packing and even humming a little, making sure that the prisoners upstairs or anybody passing by on the street heard him.

"Joe, I am leaving," Collier said as he put his arms through his coat's sleeves. There was no answer from the turnkey's room at the rear of the jail. Collier did not expect there would be, and it annoyed him that Leavell was disrespectful and stupid. He had argued with Harmonson over Leavell's role this evening and finally had given in. Leavell would remain at the jail and seem to cooperate with the mob. If there were any errors and anybody found out, nobody would believe Leavell, and he would be a convenient person to blame for letting the mob into the jail.

Collier shook his head. "I am going, Joe," he yelled again with the door half open. "Make sure you keep locked up and armed." Again there was no response, and Collier stepped out into the boardwalk. The air was drier since Wallace's funeral, but no warmer. Winter always came late to the southern plains—some rain, but mostly wind and ice. Tonight there were no clouds, which meant the temperature would drop even more. Tom shivered at the thought and pulled his gloves on. He should stop one time at Jeffery's, but the hour was late and he wanted to be at Mrs. Wallace's house and in her spare bed before another hour passed. Besides the chill, some of the mob could be at the saloon. Considering the night's work, they might be in their cups and act a little chummy with him. Better to go on to the widow's and leave them to their tasks.

—◆—

There were voices in George's dream. Some of them angry and some just mean—all were self-righteous. The voices were coming for him. His family was not there, except for Charley, who kept saying for him to wake up, wake up, WAKE UP!

George sat up in bed. Despite the cold, he felt sweaty. Collier had denied them another blanket and placed them in the other cell when they were returned to jail. He thought he was by himself until he turned and saw his brothers standing at the cell door, looking toward the stairs. Elly stood by George's bunk due to the shackles. George did not have a timepiece; he knew it must be well after midnight. Charley was looking back at him, shaking his head.

"You need to shake the sleep off, big brother. There is a mob downstairs coming for us." And Charley turned back to look at the door. George's first instinct was that he was still sleeping, and he almost lay back down until he heard the footsteps coming up the stairwell. He got completely out of bed and stood with his brothers. They had all been depressed since the capture and seemed resolved to let circumstances take their course.

"What is the plan?" George asked no one, even though all knew the question was directed at Charley. Charley did not answer and continued staring at the door. The noises were coming more quickly now, and the steel door would open any moment. In the back of the cell was a lone pewter plumbing pipe for the downstairs toilet. Nobody had understood why a pipe needed to be upstairs for a downstairs watercloset. Charley had been playing with it over the days and had gotten it loose. He had started to rip it from the walls, yet could not convince himself of a good reason to do so and despised vandalism, so he contented himself with loosening it just a bit. Now he walked over and kicked the pipe, which barely moved. He kicked again and again, and as he heard the steel door open, the pewter pipe, about three inches around and twenty inches long, fell to the floor.

On the other side of the steel door, Joe Leavell pulled the keys from the lock. There were people on the stairs behind the turnkey, whom the brothers sensed as well as heard. Feet shuffling, a muttered cough. Leavell seemed nervous and focused, both of which were rare for him. He normally closed the door behind him. This time, however, he left it open just a crack. Leavell took a step and then hooked his keys to his waistbelt, walked closer to the bars, and stood away from the steel door. Then he just stood there and looked at the brothers. It was almost like he was in one of the medicine shows that came through town and had forgotten what he was supposed to do next. He glanced at the door and back to the cell. The brothers returned the stare warily and likewise did not speak; Charley held the pipe behind his back. The men watched each other, and the silence was ended by someone on the stairs, just out of the light, swearing and then standing in the door. He was wearing well-worn clothes and had a grain sack over his head with holes that looked like they had been burned through for his eyes and mouth. He drew his gun and pointed it at Leavell.

"Unlock the cell door," the man in the grain sack said. Joe nodded, then his face betrayed that he had forgotten the next step. The brothers all suspected that the gun on Leavell was for show. Leavell stepped over to the cell and placed the key in the lock and turned it.

He did not open the door, and he stood back immediately out of the way of the gunman and the brothers.

"Charley, there is someone here to see you," Leavell said

Charley nudged Alf, and the two started walking toward the door. They might take him, right after he brained a couple at least. George stopped Charley.

"Charley, don't you see it is a mob?—for they are disguised. It is a mob, Charley." And Charley stopped. George had momentarily dropped his mantle of leadership and yelled to Leavell.

"We are entitled to security! Where is the sheriff?" Leavell did not answer or even acknowledge the statement. George even found himself looking desperately toward the hooded man for an explanation. He tried again.

"Good God, men, we are defenseless—we have been thrown in this hole without charge. The killing of Wallace was regretted by all of us. We liked the man, for he had been good to us while we were under his supervision." George knew reason would not work, so he had resorted to pleading. He could not imagine a worse end for his family. The mob came alive at the inaction of their leader, and several men forced their way into the narrow room. They were all masked, and George could smell the alcohol from the cell. He saw no ropes. That was no matter. Ropes could be outside, or they might even just shoot the brothers down in their cell. Charley had heard that Collier was blaming him for the death of Wallace, and he took his brother's place at the front.

"What do they want with me, Leavell?"

"I do not know what they want. Come out and see," the turnkey answered and backed farther away from the mob and the cell.

There were so many men in the room that there was barely enough space for them all. George suspected there were more mobsters downstairs and no doubt some watching the street out front. George was standing with both his hands on the bars. One of the mob moved quickly to the cell and placed his gun through the sidebars against George's back. George remained calm.

"If you mean to kill me, shoot me in the face and not in the back."

"I will not kill you if you will put Charley Marlow out the door."

George turned his head away from the gunman and looked at Leavell. "Every night I have laid here and wanted water, and when I begged for water you said that the keys were in the office. You said you could not get the water for me, and now you, with keys, let men in here to kill us all." Leavell responded with a look somewhere between confusion and feigned nervousness. He did not answer.

"Leavell is here under arrest," the mob leader answered.

P. A. Martin had stood silently in the rear of the mob. He had not spoken, as he was sure the Marlows would recognize his voice, in case any one of them lived. But with the indecision of the mob and the brothers not cooperating, he felt the whole deal was going bad. He wished Harmonson were here. He was better at seeing that things got done. Better than anyone P. A. knew. If no one else would act, then he would. Martin grabbed a lantern and moved toward the cell. He held it up near the bars and yelled, "Here is some light to see where to shoot Charley." Someone else at the back of the crowd yelled, "Rush them, rush Charley the hell out of there!"

The man who held the gun at George's back pulled away and moved toward the cell door, which was still closed. Charley saw the rush and stepped as far away from his brother as the chain would allow. He still held the sewer pipe behind his back. The mob member made it to the door, with most of the others gathering behind him. He pulled open the cage and stepped inside. As soon as he put his foot into the cage, Charley swung the lead pipe as hard as he could. The mobster saw it coming and managed to jerk his head back enough that the blow did not connect with all of Charley's strength and rage. What did connect served well. The force of the blow knocked the mobster back out of the cage and hard into the cell across the passage. His head smashed full with the iron bars, and then he slid down hard to the floor. For once, the mob was silent, and all eyes were on the grounded mobster. He sat there silent with his head bowed for a moment, shaking it from side to side. In his mind he had grabbed Charley and pulled him outside the cell. Then the warm fluid appeared on his hood and the pain reminded him that he had failed. He let out a moan and put both his hands on the sides of his head. "Take me out of here. I am hurt, I am bleeding to death." Then he slumped over on his side. Everybody saw the bloody spot in back of his hood where he had hit the bars, not in front where Charley had hit him.

Nobody moved except Charley, who had grown tired of admiring his work. He stepped out and grabbed the cell door and closed it behind him. George whispered to Charley, "Charley, do not ever leave your cell." Some of the mob lifted their wounded fellow, and four of them carried him out of the room and to the stairs. That made the numbers more even as best George as could count. Of course the mob was still armed—well armed, and there were probably more outside.

The remainder of the mob stood around a bit confused. Possibly it was one of their leaders that was hurt, at least George hoped so. P. A. Martin saw that the plan had turned to disaster. He grabbed one of the mob and pushed him toward the cell. "Go inside the cell and get them." The mobster stepped away from Martin's grasp and said, "I ain't going in there and get killed with that pipe." And none of them moved. It was like a bad play where the actors had not rehearsed enough. The mobster who had just spoken holstered his gun and walked out past the remainder and down the stairs. One by one, the remaining men did likewise, till a hooded Martin and Leavell were the only ones outside the cell.

Leavell walked over to the cell, pulled his keys, and turned the lock. He reached up and tested it by pulling on the cage, then walked out himself. Martin stood alone, straining through the two cutouts in his cowl to see the brothers who were looking back at him. He muttered something the brothers could not hear and walked out as well.

⸺✦⸺

Boone stood up as tall as he could in his stirrups, which was not too high. He could smell water and knew he was close to the Red. He also knew the Red's south side was all bluff with a forty-foot drop to the bottom, and he did not want to ride over it at night. He had ridden across country and stayed clear of towns, traveling at night, and had even tried to grow a beard, though it was mostly a disappointment. He knew there was a ford somewhere, because he had just passed Burkburnett. He had lost his sense of where the road should be. There was no moon, and a bit of clouds obscured any light from the stars.

His first night out, he thought every sound was from a bounty hunter, and he had slept little the day following. The farther he got away from the Brazos, the more the land cleared out, and it was hard to find any place to lie down out of sight. He had awayed the time thinking of where to go once he escaped. He mulled over Colorado and New Mexico. Home, he wanted to go home. Back to the territory. No one would be expecting him that far north, and he would stay away from soldiers and the agencies. Once across, he would head toward Susan Harboldt, his former girlfriend. They had not spoken in some time, but surely she would not turn him away. Besides, her family was used to tumbling with the law and her brothers had spent some time in jails. They might help too.

Boone's horse stumbled. *She is tired,* he thought, and it was almost dawn. He dismounted and felt his legs almost give way. He had not been afoot in hours. He led the horse around for a while and, convinced there was no road or house nearby, prepared for bedding down. He did not risk a hobble with the horse and tethered the mare to some chaparral.

While he waited for her to cool off, he lay out his own roll. It was not much, and he relied on a single blanket and his coating for warmth. The wet horse blanket he placed on another tree to dry. Once the mare was cool, he grained her with what little he had left and then poured some of his own water into the feedbag for her to have as well. He might have to risk crossing during the light. There was quicksand and other hazards on the Red. That was what he would do. Wake in a few hours and find a place to cross, and then he would be safe, or at least safer. He left his hat on to keep out some of the chill, lay down, and went to sleep listening to his horse pull at the mesquite. Even under these circumstances, he felt better than he had in a long time.

CHAPTER 15

FEDERAL JUDGE A. P. MCCORMICK'S HOME
GRAHAM, TEXAS

Ed Johnson thought about riding over to the judge's house but was glad he had walked the two blocks. It was still cold, even though the norther had blown out and the weather cleared somewhat. Johnson had heard about the aborted lynching within minutes of its failure. Collier had shown up at his house out of breath and half-dressed. All an act, Johnson supposed. Collier told the story and even how he had found lynch ropes in the tree over Wallace's grave in the cemetery. Collier was a part of it, Johnson was sure. Johnson had taken the barons' money and forged warrants, but he had never allowed any men in his custody to be harmed, that was that. Even if some innocent man he had arrested was caused to swing, it would be from a judge's order. Legal and carried out proper, not in the dark like cowards. Besides, the men he brought in might be innocent of specific charges, but they were definitely guilty of something. When able, Johnson preferred selecting his fugitives from have-nots like the Marlows. It had been fine until Collier interfered and got carried away. He should have realized the bastard was making him look bad in front of the barons. Well, now they would see who really ruled the roost.

Johnson stood on the road outside of the judge's house. He wiped off his boots on the backsides of his pants legs and wished he had shaved before rushing over. He did not even have time to cook up a good story. It was little matter; the Marlows were under arrest for state warrants and were in the custody of the county. He had little to do with it.

The town fathers had built the judge this nice two-story planta-tion home to convince him to move his bench to Graham from Dallas about ten years prior. It had worked. The judge moved, and so the seat of federal jurisprudence for most of the Indian Territory was in Graham. And he had a nice home. Johnson opened the iron yard-gate and walked over the lawn to the front porch. He leaned over to one of the windows and checked his appearance again, then knocked on the door. He had thought of the bell, but his mother had always told him, "Strangers ring, friends knock." He hoped she was correct. The judge was litigious and did not care for Johnson as one of his enforcers of the bench. Johnson also suspected the judge realized that he was in the hire of the barons. Of course, if the judge were to act on it, he would have to punish almost every federal law in Texas. They all took pay from someone, since the government did not provide it.

Johnson waited and knocked again. Then he heard something above him, then someone coming down the stairs. The door opened and it was the judge, still fastening his robe over his nightshirt. The judge looked disappointed at Johnson.

"Good morning, sir," Johnson offered and took off his hat.

"Um, good morning, Deputy. What do you need?" The judge always refused to call Johnson "marshal," since he was only a deputy marshal. It had bothered Johnson initially, but he had left it behind him.

"Judge, the Marlows, the prisoners from the territory, who killed Wallace—"

"Who are *alleged* to have killed Wallace, and only one of them at that. I doubt the county's conspiracy charge will hold for the others," the judge corrected. "Continue," he added. Johnson realized that the judge was not going to invite him in. He heard a woman inquire of McCormick from up the stairs; the judge ignored her.

"Continue, Deputy," the judge reminded.

"Yes, sir. My err. Anyway, a mob tried to lynch those boys last night, and I do not think they are safe in the jail." And Johnson recounted the story to the judge, who remained in the doorway and nodded, asking a question occasionally.

"Can you arrange transport to Dallas, with security?"

"Yes, sir. I will deputize the men myself." The judge nodded and said he would let him know later in the day what his decision was, then mumbled his thanks and closed the door. Johnson turned and walked back across the lawn to the street. He felt good about himself. With one visit he had upped the barons, and there was nothing they could do about it.

By the time he reached the jail, he was in an even better mood and more rehearsed. This time he did not bother with knocking or scraping the road off his boots. He just walked in and down the hall. He saw Collier coming down the stairs.

"I just thought you should know the judge is considering moving your prisoners to Dallas," Johnson said. Collier did not reply, merely looked at Johnson and stepped down off the last step. He put his hand in his pocket and blinked. Johnson had rehearsed a reply for Collier but continued as if it was said. "Your jail is no longer safe."

Collier looked down at the ground and thought about what he should tell the barons. He must delay. "I cannot make arrangements before tomorrow," Collier replied finally.

"Your arrangements are not necessary. I will make them myself. All I need you to do is turn them over to me when I ask for them."

"When will that be?" Collier hoped for information.

"Do not concern yourself with that. I will inform you, and I will travel with my own deputies." Johnson turned to leave but could not resist one more comment. "It was your negligence that caused Wallace's death and probably led to the mob last night. I did not care for the man, but he was never careless."

"I have done no worse than you did by bringing these men to this place. Wallace knew it too," Collier defended.

"Expect my message soon. I will need provisions for them for their trip to Dallas." And Johnson turned and walked out, leaving Collier with his biggest problem since picking up a dead man's badge.

———— ◆ ————

Boone was wrong. Susan Harboldt was not happy to see him and did not recollect as fondly as he did their past. She saw him riding up and went back to her sweeping. The closer he got to the cabin, the harder she swept the front porch. When he finally pulled up, she did not even look up or inquire about him. She just said that there were papers out on him and he could sleep in the barn for one night, then he would have to move on. She put the broom against the wall and walked into her house.

And that was that, until her brothers found out he was back. Both were older than Boone and had never taken to him or his family. Mother Harboldt had passed several years ago while the children were little better than adolescents. They had been wild before, but not compared to what they became once their mother departed. At the funeral,

Boone believed the woman had a smile on her face. Susan had done her best to take over her role but had mostly failed. Once the brothers found out he was in the barn, they scolded their sister and invited him in to supper with a pallet on the floor for sleeping. They also told him he could stay as long as he wanted. Not in the barn, on the floor of the main room of the house. Almost like he was family. The two brothers, the whole family as far as Mother Marlow was concerned, had always strayed from the law whenever practicable. Boone believed them neither honest nor dishonest, merely independent. Which was how he fancied himself.

The meal was a banquet as far as Boone was concerned, even though it was only pork shoulder and some cornbread. The pig was a bit rare and could not compare with his mother's. He enjoyed it just the same. There was talk at the table and the Harboldt brothers inquired about Boone's brothers and his mama. Boone did not recall them ever being interested before, but maybe he did not remember right. He answered as best he could and had a fine time. Every attempt at bringing Susan into the conversation failed. She would give one-word answers and look at her victuals, which she hardly touched.

After the meal, the brothers asked Boone out to the porch and left their sister to the cleaning. The house faced south, and if they kept their coats on, they would stay warm outside the wind. Once outside, he could hear Susan clanking plates and cups, telegraphing her emotions. But with a full belly and soft bedding for the next few nights, Boone was indifferent. Besides, his notoriety seemed to have raised his esteem in her brothers' eyes. They never talked of the trouble in Graham, but he knew they knew.

After they had finished several hours of talk, one of the brothers offered to get Boone's traps and lay out his pallet. He had never been waited on before and was obliged. The other kept him on the porch and even offered him a pull and some of his tobacco. Once the bed was made, Boone made his goodnights and excused himself. The blankets were placed next to the fire, and Boone climbed into the covers and, warmed by a fire for the first time in over a month, fell to sleep.

Boone waked slowly, opening his eyes and then shutting them again for a few more minutes of slumber. He smelled breakfast cooking and smiled. Maybe all this trouble would soon be over and life could be like this. Of course, his mother would never tolerate sleeping late—she would quote Proverbs and say, "A little sleep, a little slumber, and poverty shall come up on you like a curse." Boone smiled again and wondered how his mother was and if she would be upset at him for going to the Harboldts. He thought she would and reminded himself not to tell her.

He got up, rolled up his traps, and put them behind the woodpile next to the hearth. It would not do for passersby to see spare kit lying about—that might make them suspicious. Then he wandered into the kitchen. Susan was there by herself. By the dirty plates he could see that breakfast was already over and she was cooking something for him. Maybe she was fond of his courting, after all. Maybe her brothers had talked to her about him.

"Good morning. Did I miss breakfast?"

"Yes. But I am cooking some more for you," she answered distantly. Boone knew then that she was being an obliging hostess and was no longer interested.

"Thankee. I am sorry to trouble you and your family. Where are your brothers?"

"They had to pick up some supplies at the fort. They will be back for dinner or before." She took the pan off the heat and scooped the contents onto a speckled plate. Then she reached over and poured some coffee into a cup. With Boone watching, she carried both over to the table and walked back across the room, wiping her hands on her skirt.

"There is your breakfast. Sugar is on the table. We are out of salt. I have some chores to do." And she walked out of the kitchen and then out of the house. She did not even stop to put on a shawl or bonnet to keep out the cold. Boone felt awkward but sat down to eat and hoped her brothers got back soon so he would have somebody to talk to.

Noon passed and the brothers had not returned. Susan had not either. Boone expected her to at least come in out of the wind and get warm. He wanted at least some time to try to talk with her. He did not mind being rebuffed; still, he could not abide her hard feelings, at least not without explanation. He had expected her to warm up a little bit. He tried to busy himself and cleaned off his blankets and guns. He thought about warming some water and cutting himself a bath but he did not want to surprise her if she came in, or take advantage of his hosts. A bath might seem forward. Late in the afternoon, well past dinner, he heard the brothers' buckboard pull up in front of the cabin.

The buckboard was empty except for a few items. To Boone it seemed an odd trip to make for so few supplies, but maybe not everybody rationed their trips as well as his family. He had wanted to help them unload but saw that it was unnecessary. He walked out on the porch to greet them and be polite; he was their guest, after all.

"Hidy," Boone said when he walked out. The two brothers were standing by the wagon, looking at the contents in the back. They both jumped a little when he spoke.

"Why, Boone, you just startled me out of a year's growth," the older one said. The younger one grinned at Boone and nodded in agreement.

"Do you need any help?"

"No, sir. We have got it just fine, just a few things for my sister. You know how women are about the cooking things. We will bring it in directly. Go on inside out of the wind and get ready for supper. I expect Susan will have it soon." Boone nodded and gave a little wave and walked back inside.

Susan returned from her daylong chores and began preparing a late lunch. Boone walked in and tried to help, but the three of them shooed him out. "Our mama will turn over in her grave if she were to see company helping out. You go back and sit down for a while and we will call when dinner is ready," the older one said. Boone sensed he was nervous about something, despite his friendliness. True to his word, dinner was soon ready, and Boone was hungry. When he got to the table, all the plates were served, which struck Boone as odd, but then he had not supped with many families outside his own, so maybe it was proper. He pretended not to notice so he would not appear rude. The family waited until Boone sat down before they did.

"My goodness, I could eat a hoss," Boone said.

"Well, it is not horse and my sister is quite a cook." The other brother grinned and nodded again. Susan did not speak. She kept her head down while she stirred her food, which seemed to Boone the same she had done the night before.

"Eat up, Boone. There is plenty," the older one said and scooped up a healthy spoonful of the potatoes. Boone smiled and began eating. The food was not as tasty as the night before or this morning. He must have still been hungry, because he did not stop to chew much. He had always had a good appetite and the cold weather made it stronger. After several gulps he began to feel odd, and he noticed none of his hosts were eating. They were watching him, even Susan, who was crying just a bit. Why was she crying? Did someone say something to hurt her feelings? Boone hoped it was not him; he prided himself on not being rude. The feeling would not go away, and he began to think that if he put his face into his plate, then he might feel better. The room began to spin. He would just lay his face down into his plate of food, and then he would feel better. He hoped his hosts would not think him rude.

CHAPTER 16

JEFFERY'S SALOON
GRAHAM, TEXAS

*I*t was noon, and Columbus Frank Harmonson stood in the back room in front of the barons, with his hat in his hand. He felt like he was back in school and the teacher was upset at him for ciphering wrong. P. A. Martin had already explained what went wrong with the mob. Now Collier was reading Judge McCormick's order to move the prisoners to Dallas. He knew that he would receive the brunt of the barons' ire. He could tell by their expressions that the news was not well received. He kept his face down, wanting to avoid eye contact with any of them.

Harmonson was right. As soon as Martin and Collier were dismissed, the barons started in on him. There would be no more delegation. He, Harmonson, would take care of this embarrassment personally. There would be no more errors in judgment. He was asked if he understood. Harmonson said he did and was told to get out. He excused himself and stepped out of the back room.

Jeffery's was mostly empty. A few drunks and a drummer were all the outside business this day. Harmonson had never been so humiliated in his life. Since being told about the abortive lynching, he had gone over and over the plans and did not understand how fifteen armed men could fail to roust four shackled brothers out of a jail. Worse, one of the mobsters was dead, and he had been a favorite nephew of one of the barons. That had not gone over well either; Harmonson made Martin tell them about that.

It was true he was a visionary, but fools surrounded him. The barons were correct in asking him to take personal charge; it showed they retained some faith in him. That at least was comforting. He would be the leader on this next mission, and there would be no mistakes. Maybe it was true that if something needed doing, it was best to do it yourself. Maybe Christ had been right after all.

✦

The two brothers loaded Boone's body onto the buckboard. He was easier to move stiff, sort of like a door. They had waited until evening, to be sure no one saw. They had moved him to the floor as soon as he died, so that when the mortis set in he would be stiff standing up rather than sitting down. Susan cleaned the stew off his face and out of his ears and hair. They had purchased the only arsenic to be found in Fort Sill, telling the storekeeper it was for a varmint problem, and he obliged them with no questions. After that it was a simple matter of Susan mixing it in with his supper. The man at the store said it had no taste.

Once in the wagon, the older brother covered Boone's body with a blanket, not out of a sense of propriety but for security, and then placed their saddles on top of the blanket. They would sell the wagon in Graham and purchase horses to ride back. The two men climbed up onto the seat, and Susan went inside the dogtrot. Her job was to sort through his traps and determine their worth. Anything that could be identified as Boone's they would burn; the rest would be sold or traded.

They met no traffic on the way to Hell Roaring Creek. It was overcast and cold, so the sounds would not travel far. Not that anyone living in the area would mind a few gunshots in the evening. They parked the wagon on the bluff over the creek, which was dry and would remain so until spring or early summer. They lifted the wagon's gate and positioned themselves at either end of the body and noticed how light he seemed since he had died. The younger one was sure that was because his soul had left.

They looped a *lazo* under his arms and lowered him over the bank. Light or not, it took a few minutes to position the body upright against the cut. The top of his head was just several inches below the bank's edge. The younger brother placed their only lantern above him on the flat.

"Can you make him out?" he asked back to his elder. They had been concerned not to fire too close so that there would be no powder burns on him. A desperado as bad as Boone Marlow would never allow himself to be taken alive or shot close. His brother aimed the Colt's at arm's length and closed one eye and then the other, trying to capture the proper sight picture. He had never been too smooth with handguns and thought about letting his brother shoot.

"That is fine. Step back on outta there," the elder said, and he motioned his brother back with the pistol.

"Where are you going to shoot him at, in the guts or the head?" the younger asked, scrambling off the creek's embankment and trotting over to his brother. His brother kept aiming and changing eyes and position.

"Why, in the head! We are dangerous *pistoleros,* and this will let everyone know it. Now hush so I can get my aim."

"Do not shoot the lantern, it is the only one I brung." The elder lowered his gun and looked at his brother. "I reckon I can hit a dead man in the head from twenty feet—now shut up!"

He raised his arm, aimed, and fired, hitting Boone in the head. Before he could adjust for a second shot, the body slid into the creek. "Shit," the younger said, and he went and straightened the body up again. Once in place, he examined his brother's marksmanship. "Hey, you got him between the eyes."

"Well, back off, and I will do another." The younger nodded and scurried back alongside his brother. The elder aimed and fired again. This time Boone slipped a bit but remained upright. Both men walked up to check the holes. The elder checked his chamber in case he needed to shoot again. The younger grabbed the lantern and held it front of Boone's face.

"Two holes, right in the forehead," he said, proud of his big brother. "Did you notice there is no blood?"

"Forget about that. No one will ever notice. Just let me do all the talking. Let us get him back into the wagon and start for Graham." And they hoisted him up on the bank and then into the wagon. The younger did his best to figure how much the reward would be, since they were bringing him in dead and there would be no trial. He knew it would be some less but hoped there was still enough to buy his sister the new dress she wanted for her cut in the deal.

CHAPTER 17

*J*t was almost 8:00 P.M. The brothers heard the voices and footfalls on the stairs. There was no anger or stress to them, and they remained on their bunks shackled together in pairs. Charley's hat lay on the floor between them, and the foursome took turns tossing cards into the crown. No one mentioned what their mother would say if she saw them with the deck. The only news they had heard was from Leavell, who said the fella that Charley had dough-popped died of brain fever. That had put them in an even more somber mood. The steel door opened, and Ed Johnson and a man they did not recognize stepped through. The boys looked up from their game.

"Boys, get ready fast. I have orders to take you to Weatherford tonight. Nobody knows about it except me and my guards."

"Who are your guards?" Alf asked.

"Three of mine and three from Collier."

George answered before anyone else could. "It is a mob either way, but we will probably stand a better chance outside than in here."

Johnson grunted, "Go ahead and get ready, quick." He turned and walked off, insulted. George felt bad about the remark and knew Johnson had no part in the mob actions, though he was responsible for their initial arrest. The brothers gathered up what few belongings they had and were led, stumbling with their shackles, downstairs by the unknown man.

As they came down the stairs they heard the familiar chatter of men, which stopped as soon as they came into view. There were at least fifteen men gathered around the main office and in the corridor.

George looked around and counted, then eyed his brothers and shook his head. "I guess he was wrong about 'nobody' knowing."

Charley caught Johnson's eye, "You lied to us, Ed." The marshal did not respond as the brothers were escorted down the corridor and onto the street. Outside were twenty to thirty more citizens.

"Ed, you are taking us out to have us mobbed again," Charley said as he was helped up onto the back of the buckboard with his brothers.

"Nobody will run on us with my guard," Johnson said, busying himself with the prisoners' placement.

"If they do, will you give us guns?" Charles asked.

"Yes, and die with you, if it comes to that." Johnson was lying and Charley knew it.

"It is mighty easy to talk, Johnson, but will you do it?" Alf asked.

"I will." The brothers noticed he had said that loud enough for all the men to hear.

There were two wagons, a buckboard with the prisoners, driven by P. A. Martin, and a four-passenger surrey for the deputies. The deputies' driver came over to the prisoners' wagon. "What say we run a rope through their irons and fasten them to the back?" the driver said.

"Not necessary," the marshal replied. Then he walked back to the deputies' wagon and climbed aboard in the messenger seat. Martin turned around, and Johnson gave him a wave to tell him to move out. There were no clouds, and it would be a cold ride to Weatherford. George leaned forward a bit and noticed some blankets gathered around Martin's feet.

"It is pretty dern cold. Why don't you want that blanket over your lap?" George asked.

"I do not want it in my way," Martin answered.

Martin stirred the team ahead of the deputies' wagon, and they made their way out of Graham quickly. The lights were on in the few buildings they passed on the outskirts, but nobody was outside. A mile away from the jail, Martin turned the buckboard onto the Finis road toward Weatherford. The brothers kept looking back and had lost sight of the deputies altogether.

"You had better slow down. The guards are not coming," George said.

"They will catch up pretty soon," Martin answered, uninterested in his opinion.

"We will be mobbed in fifteen minutes," Charley said to his brothers. Hearing this, Martin eased the team back and tried to whistle, but it was too cold. The brothers could tell he was shivering and did not have on a heavy coat. Not one heavy enough to carry him all the way to Weatherford and back in January.

About two miles outside of Graham, they heard the guard wagon closing behind them, and Martin stopped the buckboard and set the brake on the near side of a dry creek. To their right was a heavy wood-line on both sides of the creek; on their left were several cultivated fields. The guards pulled alongside, and Johnson got out.

"Maybe the boys need something to warm them up, Marshal. Boys, have a drink," Martin said, entirely too loud for their close environs.

Charley whispered, "That shout was a signal. Get ready, boys. This is where they intend to kill us." P. A. Martin pulled a flask from his coat and handed it to Johnson, who pulled and then passed it back to the brothers. Each took a small sample and then each spat it out silently on the floor of the buckboard. They wanted their wits about them. The guards had all piled out of their vehicle and were waiting a turn at the bottle.

"Halt! I say halt!" A man had stepped out of the brush on the far side of the ford and was leveling a rifle. The moon was not up, yet his silhouette could be made out. His voice sounded muffled, as if he had a scarf over his face. Nobody moved. The bottle had been handed back to Johnson, who dropped it. The glass shattered the silence begun by the assassin's challenge. P. A. Martin knew this was the time. He sprang from the wagon, followed by the guard riding next to him, and ran for the tree line, yelling, "Here they are—take all of the bastards!" And they disappeared into the night.

As Martin and the deputy cleared the vehicle, several masked men stepped from the treeline and opened fire on the prisoners. Yelling and running, the gunmen rushed the wagon bearing the brothers. The guards jumped off their vehicle and followed Martin into the woods. Johnson reacted from instinct and pulled his revolver and began to take aim. Before he had sighted, a bullet splintered his only hand, and he dropped the weapon and fell to the ground. "There are guns in this wagon, boys, fight for your lives!" Johnson yelled at the brothers, who began piling out of the buckboard.

The brothers ran in their shackled pairs to the deputies' surrey. The driver who had wanted to rope them into the wagon, no doubt for easier shooting, was still on the reins, trying to hold the skittish team through all the gunfire. Johnson got up and was trying to get control of his revolver. A hooded man from the woods ran up behind Johnson and grabbed him, trying to wrestle away his pistol from his wounded hand. Charles and Elly leapt from the buckboard at the hooded man and got Johnson's revolver, and Charles pointed it into the mobster's groin.

"Do not shoot. I am a guard," the man pleaded.

"Let loose, then." And Charley cocked the piece. The man let go of the pistol and longarm and ran back into the woods where he had come from. George and Elly went for the surrey driver, who froze as the two ran up on him and allowed them to take his pistol and Winchester before jumping out. The driverless team ran into the creek, flipping the wagon over. Johnson, satisfied he had done his duty, scurried over to the road ditch and took cover, crimping his wounded hand under the armpit.

The brothers formed a circle in the road next to the remaining wagon. The horse was stirred, but the brake set and the vehicle would not move. George patted the horse's croup and made calming noises to the animal to convince it to stay. They needed the buckboard as a wall against the mob and maybe to escape in. They knew they made a target in the road but were afraid to move in any direction, not knowing where the mob was.

It was quiet, and the brothers could hear themselves breathing, the steam escaping. Just then one of the braver mobsters rushed from the treeline, yelling and shooting. Charley did not even aim the weapon and hit him on the fly. The man dropped to the ground and was silent. Charley was unsure whether he had killed him or not. He did not want to spend another bullet.

The brothers stared at the man, still on the road, and did not notice that all the mobsters had stepped out of their hiding and were in a circle around them. The mob began screaming and firing at once. The darkness off the road was filled with flashes of light. Bullets plunked into the wagon, sending splinters, and dirt from missed shots into the road spurted around the brothers' feet. The dray would not be still, and George did not want to lose their fort. They must return fire. Instinctively the brothers knelt down and returned fire; all they could aim at were the flashes of light and brief silhouettes. The brothers' returned fire was sufficient, and the mob circle moved back into the safety of the woods. The Marlows could see one more body on the road, moaning and crawling toward the ditch. A third had also been hit, and he stood in the road cursing and holding his arm. A mobster ran from the trees and pulled him to safety.

All was quiet again. Originally the guns were ice cold in the brothers' hands. Now they were warmed, and this helped them against the chill. The sound of their steamed breath returned. They thought about taking ammunition from the body a short distance away, but all were dread to move. Three mobsters darted from the woods and fired into the brothers. George was hit in the arm, causing him to drop his rifle. Alf fired back till his pistol was empty, then leaned over to pick the Winchester off the ground. While bent over, it looked like Alf had only lost his balance and fell, but he did not move once he was on the ground. Charley leaned over and nudged him. Alf was dead. Charley wanted to cry out but did not want to let the mob know their bullets had found a target. He looked over at his other two brothers. Elly was down and George was leaning over him, holding Elly's head in his hands.

"Elly, can you get up?" George asked.

"No, I can never get up anymore." And Elly died too.

Charley heard no firing and no movement in the brush, just his brother George's sobs. He had never heard his brother cry before. It sounded strange. George had taken his father's place after his death and had always been strong. It was sad to Charley to listen to George's crying, and it kept him from thinking about his two dead siblings in the road. Then George stopped crying, picked up his rifle with his good arm, and cradled it the best he could with his wounded limb. He began firing into the woods and yelling like a madman. Charley pitched in too. If this was how it was going to end, at least they would go standing up and not at the end of a rope. Charley had always figured he would die in bed.

"There are some of them," George said and he leveled his weapon toward the guard's overturned surrey stuck down in the creek. There were some men moving around, though no fire had come from there.

"Do not shoot down there. They are the guards," Charley cautioned. And with that warning, a shotgun blast from behind the surrey hit Charley Marlow in the face and shoulder. He did not feel or hear it, only saw it, and then his legs gave way. George yelled again and fired his remaining rifle shots into the vehicle.

And it was quiet again. George tried to lift Charley to his feet or at least get him to sit up but he could not. Charley, bleeding badly, his face covered in blood, was still breathing. And George was all alone.

The mob had taken its licks as well. The night was cold, and several of them were down or wounded. Many started to leave. There was no meeting called or retreat sounded, but many of the men, angered over the death of Wallace, now felt vindicated enough to go home. There it was warm and nobody would shoot at them. George was tired and wanted it to end.

"Come again, you cowardly bastards! We have plenty of ammunition and nobody hurt. Come on!" George yelled from the center of the road with his three brothers lying around him. He wanted to join them, and he was going to oblige the mobsters to join them as well. But there was silence, not even movement in the trees or the creek.

Columbus Frank Harmonson was getting mounted when he heard the shouting from the road. He had not tried to get the mob to stay and was ready to go himself; then he heard the last brother yelling. He knew the other three were dead or dying and had convinced himself that his work was done. He was not sure but believed he had even shot one of the brothers himself. He sat on the horse and listened and noticed no one else was going back; then he remembered himself. He had never left a job undone. As soon as the firing started, he had sent one of the supposed guards riding back into town with the word that Boone Marlow and a gang were ambushing the guards. That story would do fine, but there was still one man left. How hard could it be to shoot to death four men shackled together in the middle of a road? Harmonson cursed himself for his laziness and dismounted, ashamed. He began walking up toward the road. P. A. Martin had been mounted with him and called out.

"Where are you going?"

"Back to see it out," Harmonson replied and trudged through the scrub oak and chaparral and up to the road.

George had begun to believe the mob had left. He had heard several horses leaving and no more firing from the trees, but he kept his watch. Then he noticed a man standing on the road. He had not seen the man walk up. He had just appeared. They stared at each other. Then the man pulled his revolver and began walking and firing at George. George aimed his rifle but clicked on the empty chamber. He threw it down and pulled the pistol from his pants with his good arm. The man was undaunted and continued walking and firing. George aimed the revolver and fired two times. The man dropped and did not move. George heard some more horses and spun around to see them riding back toward Graham. And it was quiet again

George tried to remember what was going on, but he couldn't form any thoughts. He was wounded in the arm and felt the pain for the first time, then he heard his brother moan just a bit—it was Charley. George leaned over him and took his hand. Charley was conscious but bleeding badly.

"Our brothers are dead and their souls are in heaven," George said, still confused; he did not know what else to say.

"Yes, now we must get loose from them and out of here. See if you can find a knife in one of the dead mobsters' pockets." Charley wheezed and laid his head back down.

George pulled Elly with him over to the nearest body and located a large folding knife. He dragged his brother back over to where Charley lay. He started crying and told Elly he was sorry. He remembered when they were kids, Elly had fallen and got some gravel and dirt scraped under his knee. It got infected, and their pa had fixed him up. George was careful not to let Elly get hurt like that this time. He was still confused and did not know how a knife would help them now. Perhaps Charley wanted him to cut out some of the buckshot. He handed Charley the knife.

"Stand over here," Charley said and sat up a bit on his elbows, using Alf's body for a brace. George moved Elly where he had pointed. Charley pulled himself over to Elly's body and looked at him for a moment. George saw him mouth, "I am sorry" and he kissed his forehead. He then pulled back to Elly's shackled ankle and lifted the pants leg and took off the brogan and sock. He felt around until he found the joint and began sawing the foot off his brother. George did not say anything, and after Charley was finished he pulled the shackle off the stump and handed the blade to George and motioned toward Alf.

"I cannot, my hand is too shot to hold the blade, much less cut," George lied. His hand did throb, but he would not cut his little brother's foot off. Charley nodded and wheezed some more and took the knife back. He seemed to be holding back from vomiting but amputated Alf's foot as well. He did not kiss Alf but instead patted him on the chest and rubbed his hair just a bit.

George helped Charles walk to the buggy, both dragging bloody shackles, and then went around and gathered up all the weapons and ammunition he could find off his brothers and dead mobsters. He hollered for Marshal Johnson, who did not answer. Satisfied he had obtained all he could, he climbed into the buggy. There was only one place they could go. They had an obligation to tell their mother what had happened. She might even be in danger herself. George handed Charley his pistol.

"Use it if necessary."

"Drive for your life," Charley replied.

CHAPTER 18

THE FINIS ROAD
YOUNG COUNTY, TEXAS

George did not spare the horse. Charley had passed out again, and George leaned across and held him in the seat. He was finally realizing what had happened and what they had done. He did not know how many of the mob were killed; he was sure there were several at least—more than the mob had gotten of them. Charles moaned again, and George told him it was going to be all right, though he was not sure himself. The cold air had helped stem his bleeding, but the road did them no favors. He was not sure if they could make it all the way to Finis.

Just off the road, he spotted a farm with a light on. George assumed it must be after midnight and was glad someone was awake. Less chance of a bullet that way, and there had been enough shooting this night. George eased the wagon and turned into the drive leading up to the farmhouse. Charley stirred and asked for water. George braked the buckboard and hallooed into the house. There was no movement, and then he hallooed again. The door opened and an old man appeared on the porch holding a lantern; he did not leave the porch. George inquired about some water for his brother and someone to tend wounds. At the mention of wounds the old man jerked his head and hurried back into the house. As soon as he was inside, he killed his silhouette with the candle and the house was dark. No water here.

It was another hour before George arrived at Finis. He drove past his mother's and on to Denson's. There he hallooed and yelled for Mr. Denson to come to his mother's quickly; he waited for no light and turned the buckboard around for his home.

In front of the Marlow cabin, he braked hard and pulled Charles out on his side. He had lost consciousness again, and there was more blood. His coat and shirt were slick with it. As best he could with his injured arm, George toted his brother to the front porch and kicked on the door, yelling for his mama.

Martha Jane had heard the wagon arrive. She had slept lightly all her life and believed it good practice on the plains. She did not expect trouble, despite the late hour, from someone traveling in a buckboard. Problems did not come in wagons; trouble normally arrived on fast horses ridden by faster men. She threw on her dressing gown and lit a candle before she opened the door. Then she heard her eldest's voice; it was desperate, and she rushed to the door. When she opened it, George could not hold his brother any longer, and Charles fell through. She gasped and all she saw was the blood. George did not seem to pay her any mind. He just knelt down and shook Charles, then he grabbed his face in his hands.

"Charley, are you going to give up?" George demanded. Charles did not answer. George shook him again and repeated the question angrily. Charles opened his eyes and smiled a bit, "No," he said, and he kept his eyes open this time as he lay his head back.

"Help me get him onto the bed, mama."

The first rider arrived in Graham before any of the brothers had even been shot. It was a guard, and he followed his instructions to the letter. As soon as the first round was fired, he ducked out of the buggy and ran into the woods. Once there, a horse was waiting and Frank Harmonson was holding him. One last check on the instructions to make sure he understood. Ride into town and tell everyone seen that Boone Marlow's gang had ambushed the guards and in the ensuing gun battle all the brothers were dead, except Boone, who got away with his gang intact after the aborted rescue. Harmonson had him repeat it again and then sent him off.

Once in Graham he found the streets empty. All seemed retired to their homes or various saloons. The man thought about going straight to the sheriff's office, then remembered his instructions. He rode past the office and on into the square and rode up to the front of the county courthouse. Once there he pulled his revolver and fired several rounds into the air. He holstered his gun and waited.

He did not have to wait long. Several men came wandering out of the bars on the north side of the square and toward the gunfire. In Graham it was unusual to hear shots in the middle of the night, so none thought there was any danger. Several men gathered around him, some took hold of his bridle to calm the horse, who was not used to this much activity. Most of the men were drunk or on their way to being so. He was flooded with questions and held his silence until he saw Tom Collier join the crowd at the back. Right on cue, Collier asked what had happened.

"Boone Marlow and a gang has ambushed the guards. I stopped the buggy in the creek upon seeing my friends being shot down, but was prevented from firing on the mob by two men who came up on each side of the buggy. It was very hard not to be allowed to help my friends. I do not believe there is any God, or He would not allow good men to be killed that way," the man said. Then he remembered the most important part. "All the Marlows are dead except for Boone, who got away." This bit of news had the desired effect, and the crowd began yelling. Several of them started leaving to find their horses and ride out to the Finis road.

Collier nodded at the man and began walking back toward the jail. All went according to plan. Several of the men followed and were trading comments and opinions back and forth all the way to the jail. Collier's horse had remained saddled, and he got mounted and rode out himself to Dry Creek on the Finis road. He clucked his mount to get ahead of the crowd he knew would follow.

The first thing Collier noticed upon his arrival at the creek was the smell of powder that still hung low to the ground. Then he noticed the several bodies lying in the road. He got off and saw that two of the bodies were lying by themselves in the center of the road and had one foot amputated apiece. There was not too much blood because of the cold. He struck a match to see the faces. It was two of the brothers. He noticed only one of the vehicles was still present, and he started looking around for the remainder of the Marlow family. Then he heard a voice from the far side of the road in a ditch and saw someone struggling to get up. Fearing one of the brothers was still alive in the bush, he jerked his pistol and blew out the match. How could he have been so stupid to ride up to a fresh battlefield and be so careless? The voice spoke again and this time he caught it, and the figure trying to regain his feet; it was Johnson holding his one arm close to his breast.

"The other two took off. I think one of them is dead, though. Looks like your little plan failed."

"What do you mean? I had no part in this," Collier replied.

Johnson walked over to another body in the road a few yards from the dead brothers. With his wounded hand still crooked under his armpit, he toed the scarf away from the body's face; it was Frank Harmonson. Collier walked over.

"Looks like your boss is dead," Johnson said. Collier knelt down and struck another lucifer. He was in shock and did not know what to say. Two of the brothers were back on the loose, and his liaison with the barons lay dead in the road wearing the same red and black sack suit Wallace had teased him about last summer.

"I wager if you check the other bodies you will find that they are all local and not part of the guard detail. I do not think any of the guards were hit; they were running pretty fast if they were."

Collier said nothing again. He kept looking at Harmonson's face. What should he do now? He was decent at following orders, not planning. The sound of horses interrupted his thoughts. The crowds from Graham were arriving and soon there would be enough to hold a town meeting. The men from Graham had dismounted and were gathering around Frank Harmonson's body. Nobody had paid enough attention to remember that he was not a member of the guards. Johnson did not mention it again and began walking back toward Graham. He would assume no more responsibility for this. None of the Graham citizens seemed to pay him any attention.

Everyone was looking at Collier for the plan. He told them to gather up the bodies from the road and check the woods to see if there were any wounded fellows as well. The brothers and several bodies of their fellow citizens were loaded into the guards' buggy once it was recovered from the creek bed. There was not enough room, so some of them were tied to the backs of the men's horses. Once the place had been tidied up to Collier's satisfaction, he gathered all the men around. He had used the time to formulate his plan. Nobody but Johnson knew who was in the guard detail, and he had taken off on his own. He would stick to the plan; instead of killing them on the road, they would kill them in Finis, which was where he assumed they would go. Folks in trouble always seemed to head home.

"Everybody listen to me. Boone Marlow's gang has taken several of our friends to their death. I believe the two brothers are holding up at their cabin in Finis. I am deputizing all of you to ride with me there now and avenge our friends and what these people have done to our good town." He paused for dramatic effect and listened to the mood of the crowd. "Extermination of the Marlows—men, women, and children!" he yelled at last. Several of the men joined in, and soon all were on their horses. Nobody seemed to care much that there were no children to exterminate.

CHAPTER 19

❦

MARLOW CABIN
FINIS, TEXAS

*T*he Marlow house was well forted up. The cabin had been built before the Comanche were gone and the shutters still had firing holes in them. Their mother had kept her head despite being told of her two sons' death at the hands of the mob, and it was she who had come up with the plan. She had gathered plenty of foodstuffs and water while George did as much as possible with his one hand to prepare the building. Charley lay on the bed and was in charge of any reloading that would be needed. They worked fast. Denson helped for a while, but Martha Jane excused him and thanked him for his troubles, refusing to let him stay. "This is our fight," she said.

The first armed men showed up an hour after sunrise. They did not fire on the cabin and stayed well away. They made no attempt to communicate at all. After a while some of them took their ease in a cottonwood grove across the road and started a fire to make some coffee. Martha Jane took her Testament out of her poke and gathered what was left of her family around the bed for prayer. It was her husband's favorite: the Ninety-first Psalm. After she had finished, she brushed off her skirt and repeated, "His will be done."

The men outside were cold and hungry, and a few of them starting a hangover. The coffee helped some, and they were glad to get it and kept offering up suggestions of what to do. One of them wanted to take a wagon and fill it with hay, set it on fire, and push it into the cabin. No one else thought this was a good idea. Sober heads prevailed and they decided to wait on Collier, who had ridden over to Jacksboro to consult with their sheriff. Legally, Finis was in the Jack County, and

Collier wanted their laws present and agreeable before anyone started anything.

Shortly before noon, Collier arrived with about twenty more men and the Jack County sheriff. All were well armed and equipped for the task. Sheriff Moore took charge at once. He never seemed to confer with Collier and took liberty in posting his men. Also along was one Texas Ranger, who was the only person Moore seemed to communicate with. He said his name was Augberg, and he kept his own counsel, but he did let his ranger badge, made from a Mexican Peso, be seen on the outside of his mackinaw.

They posted men on all the roads and intersections as well as the woods surrounding the lonely farmhouse. After about an hour of that, Moore seemed satisfied and with Collier approached the house unarmed. He walked to about fifty feet of the front door and saw that he was covered by at least two weapons from the cabin. He raised his hands away from his body and motioned for Collier to do the same.

"I am Sheriff Moore of Jack County. If you folks fire on two unarmed peace officers it will go worse for you than it is now," Moore shouted, not unfriendly.

"No worse than what they done for us; state your business," George hollered back. It was paining him to keep the rifle aimed with his injured hand. He did not want to change to a revolver and try left-handed but thought he might.

"I would like to talk to you folks about this; all you have to do is lay down your arms and come out and you will not be harmed. You have my word," Moore solicited.

"We have talked enough. You cannot protect us from Collier's mob and we do not intend on leaving," George replied.

"Can I come in there and talk? I am unarmed," Moore responded.

"No," George snapped. "We will only allow in a doctor for my brother. Anyone else approaches this building and I will shoot them on sight."

With that the two men backed away from the cabin and toward the rest of the men. Once safe, Moore told Collier to send someone to Graham and fetch a doctor.

It took several hours for a doctor to be located. By the time he had arrived it was almost dark. Denson had been watching from his home all day long, and it was making him sick. Even though Martha Jane had politely told him that it was not his affair, Denson decided to throw in anyway. He grabbed his shotgun and walked over to the crowd where the doctor and the sheriffs were. When he arrived, there was an argument going on over jurisdiction between the two county officials. Collier had been told of the scheme to torch a hay wagon and push it into the building and liked the idea. Moore had not and wanted to know what Collier's hurry was about. Moore was not about to gun-rush a building with a woman inside. The doctor sat in his buggy, trying to stay warm, and rummaged through his bag. Denson listened for a few moments and waited for a break in the talk. He was not a loud man and was used to being paid little attention. Threats or not, he must do what is right. He did not like speaking and was always afraid at being asked to read the Psalter in Church. "Men!" he shouted. "There has been enough blood shed over this affair. Collier and his deputies have not brought you here in the interests of peace and justice, but as another mob bent on wreaking vengeance upon the Marlows, who have done nothing but defend their lives when attacked. I am tired of this," he said and waited for someone to comment. None did, and all stared at him in his overalls with no hat or coat. He began again, "I am going inside, if they will allow me, and if they will not surrender to me, I will at least see how they are. If the cabin is attacked while I am in there, you will have to kill me before you get to the Marlows. Come on, Doc, you are coming with me." And he turned and walked off. He took the first steps slowly, waiting for someone to yell at him or try and stop him. None did. He did not turn around and soon heard the doctor's footsteps trotting to catch up to him. The posse watched and saw the two men stop short of the cabin for a minute. The house was dark, but they could just hear a voice questioning them. Then the door opened and the two walked the rest of the way.

Once inside, George searched the doctor while Charley lay on the bed pointing a pistol at him. Denson lay his shotgun beside the door and had forgotten he had it and was flattered that that the brothers had allowed him to carry it into the house. After the search, the doctor mumbled, "First things first," and began dressing George's hand. George remained by the window slit, and there was little light inside for the doctor to do his work. He asked for another candle to be lit and was refused. He took a few minutes with George's hand and had it dressed quickly. He told Martha Jane how to change the dressing, whereupon she thanked him and reminded him she was a doctor's wife and knew how to nurse. He smiled and squeezed her arm and proceeded over to Charley. Denson had been asked nothing and had said nothing, just stood by the door. He could tell the family had crossed some sort of moment in life where the normal cares did not matter. The entire time he was there, none asked how many were in the posse or what their intentions were. Denson was glad and felt a bit guilty over the way he had acted, and did not want to talk anymore anyway.

When the doctor arrived at Charley, he insisted that another candle be lighted or he could not perform his duties. Before George could answer, Martha Jane produced one and lit it. She held it above Charley's wounds and stroked his hair with her other hand, being careful to stay out of the doctor's light and hands. After a few minutes of examination the doctor looked up at Martha Jane.

"I can do nothing without putting him under anaesthetic," He said and reached for his bag.

"But I do not want to be put to sleep. That mob might hit us at any moment," Charley said. The doctor kept rummaging through his bag. He did not notice George coming up behind him with a pistol until he felt the barrel on the back of his head. He stopped rummaging and did not appear scared, only irritated. Denson was embarrassed for the family. He had never seen them rude or forward before.

"Charley," George said cocking the pistol, "let him put you to sleep, and if he does not wake you when I think he ought to, I will shoot him."

"I do not think his wounds are mortal if they are treated soon. I am a doctor and not a peace officer. Madam, if you will have your son remove his weapon I can begin, unless you want to lose more children this week," the doctor said. Martha Jane nodded, and George lowered the pistol and walked back to his post. The doctor pulled out a bottle and some cotton wadding. He poured the contents of the jar onto the wads, held it underneath Charley's nose, and told him to breathe deeply.

The mood outside had passed onto boredom. Some of the men had left and others gone to sleep. A small command post had been established across the road from the cabin the cottonwoods. Collier had gotten mad and stormed off to talk with his men. What made him mad was Moore's admonition that Finis was in Jack County, and Young County officers had no jurisdiction here unless he gave it to them. The ranger had concurred, and Collier felt his tiny world go spinning out of control. He had walked over to his constituents, who were of little support. None of them would have been there if they knew the truth of the matter. Most were there because they were bored, and some because they had liked Wallace. Several were realizing there would be little excitement but were too timid to leave. For others, this was the most exciting event in the county in their lifetimes. Some had missed the war or the Indians. They were not about to miss this.

The front door to the cabin opened, then closed, and they heard the doctor halloo off the porch and announce that he was coming out alone. As soon as he was across the road, several of the men swarmed him; how many men? Was Boone in there with his gang? And so on. The doctor ignored them all and proceeded to the Jack County sheriff.

"Where is the other man who went in with you?" Moore asked.

"He is staying with the Marlows and says he will help fight the Collier crowd if he has to," the doctor replied and handed the officer a note from the family. The sheriff took the note and was joined by Collier, who had rushed over when the doctor arrived. He was not going to let Moore forget that it was his county that had been wronged and not Jack County.

Moore opened the note and Collier stuck his face over his shoulder trying to read it.

"Excuse me," Moore said, and he removed himself closer to the fire where he could get some light and some privacy. The note was barely legible but clear in purpose. The brothers would surrender peaceably to the U.S. marshal in Dallas. They had been mobbed twice and did not trust that any local officers could or would protect them.

Moore finished the note and handed it to the ranger. After he read it, he handed it back to the sheriff and shook his head. The Jack County sheriff folded the letter and put it in his breast pocket. Moore called Collier over and did not hand him the note.

"I do not think we have any right to arrest these men without a writ or warrant; they are still U.S. prisoners," Moore said.

"It is a shame to let three men back off seventy-five, unless you are afraid," Collier replied. Moore did not believe there were forty-five, much less seventy, and let the slight pass. Collier was trying to goad him into a mistake. He had made this mess, and Moore would let him keep it. Moore walked over to his horse and nodded for his men to do the same. Collier walked after him, pleading his cause. Moore remained stoic and mounted his roan.

"I am leaving it alone and sending for the U.S. marshal in Dallas. Ranger Augberg will stay here to help keep an eye on them. I do not expect there to be any foolishness in my county. This is a federal matter and I expect them to take care of it." And he rode away with the Jack County posse following.

Collier stood all alone in the cottonwoods and his small world seemed more out of control than ever. The ranger would be of no help, and soon there would be federal men all over. He saw the doctor walking toward his buggy unescorted and unnoticed. Collier ran over to him. He intended to get some information.

"How many men do they have, Doctor, and what condition are they in?" Collier asked. The doctor eased himself into his seat and put a blanket over his legs. He ignored the request. Collier asked again.

"Young man, you brought me out here to do some doctoring. I have done as requested. Now I am heading back into town and hope to get some sleep. Maybe there will not be any babies to bear in the morning, and I can get some rest and warm my bones. You will have to get someone else to do your spying for you," the doctor said and hawed the horse and walked him out onto the road heading back to Graham.

— ❖ —

The two Harboldt brothers had left their sister at home. She wanted to come and it took them a while to talk her out of it. Her real reason was to ensure her share of the reward, though she did not bring herself to say it. The trip to Graham had taken the two Harboldts several days, and they had almost lost the body twice, once in the Red and the other in the Wichita. They had arrived the night before and camped out on the Salt Fork. There were some Indians there who were afraid of men carrying a body around with them. The brothers managed to talk them out of some whiskey anyway.

When morning was several hours old, they started into Graham. They were both familiar with the town and went straight to the county courthouse. When they pulled up and parked the vehicle, there was a large crowd gathered on the front steps. The brothers set the brake and walked up to see the sight, always being curious. They excused their way through the people assembled and saw two bodies in lidless coffins displayed and leaning up against the front wall of the building. There was signage hanging and stretched between the two coffins. Neither of the men could read and had to ask what it said. A little girl obliged

them. It read: "Alfred and Lewellyn Marlow, horse thieves and murderers of Sheriff Wallace." The brothers were worried and afraid their
bounty might be in question. They hurried inside to see who they
needed to deal with about the reward for Boone, and did not notice
that their former neighbors were absent one foot apiece.

CHAPTER 20

*T*he federal laws from Dallas arrived after a few days. They had ridden to Fort Worth and then took the train to Weatherford. Once
there, they had rented a wagon and a team and drove north and west
out to Finis. The Marlows had agreed to surrender and kept their word
with one provision: that they be allowed to bury their brothers.

Martha Jane had remained stoic and determined throughout the
siege, until her dead sons were brought to her from Graham in a buckboard. Denson had been allowed to go and fetch them once the feds
showed up and agreed to the funeral. None in the posse had mentioned
that Boone was with the dead. She had not really given much thought
to Boone and thought him safe and away. Denson told her a family
named Harboldt had brought him in and tried to collect the reward,
but the doctor said he had been poisoned, then shot. He did not tell
her how the boys were displayed in town. The federal judge had the
Harboldts arrested for murder, since the crime had most likely occurred
in the territory. They had made bond, and nobody had seen them since.
Denson said he was real sorry and helped George and Charley load
their brothers into the house. Martha Jane had just stood there staring
at nothing while they gathered her dead children. She felt like dying
herself and was glad her husband had not seen this. Would it have
come to this if he were still alive? Perhaps she was not the matriarch
she tried to be. She stood out on the porch until George came and led
her inside. The boys must be readied, he told her. Denson went to his
house to find some clean towels and more soap. One of the posse,
watching from a distance, took off his hat and nodded at her.

The dead siblings were placed on the table and the brothers began undressing them. Martha Jane came inside and watched from the door. She had expected the other two, but it really did not arrive with her until she saw them in the back of that buckboard. And her baby Boone as well.

"What are you two doing?" she demanded.

George looked up from his task, "Why, Mama, we are getting them prepared."

"I want you to stop at once. Do you hear me? Stop!" And she walked over to the bodies, "My babies will get too cold in this weather, get some clothes on them and help me get them over to the fire to warm them up," she said and commenced to tidying them up. George looked at his brother. Through all of this she had been strong, and now this was too much for her, for anyone. Three dead sons and more trouble yet. She walked over to Boone and began stroking his hair. She began gently sobbing at first and then crying out loud. George and Charley just watched. They did not know what else to do. They had never seen their mama like this.

"Oh why, oh why did they disfigure your marble brow with those ugly holes?" she said to Boone's lifeless form. Then she leaned over and put her ear next to his lips.

"Who did it, my boy? Tell your old mother, please, whisper in her ear." The crying had grown stronger, and she shook Boone's body. "Your mother can hear the whisper of her boy's lips, can't you hear me, darling?" And she leaned over, fully embracing his head, and began crying again. George and Charley gentled her away from the body. She did not struggle but held her hand out to her youngest. "If there is a God, why will He allow such outrages?" The brothers led her outside and onto the porch. Denson and his wife arrived, and the brothers asked her to please take care of their mother for a while. They would clean the boys up. Charley brought her a quilt and a shawl.

After several hours, Martha Jane arrived back at the cabin. One of the federal officers had escorted her back at Mrs. Denson's request. She felt weak and ashamed. She had never let anyone see her like that, and as soon as she had come to her senses, prayed with Mrs. Denson. Her one relief was that two of her boys were safe, for the moment, and the others had been Christians and were now in their Glory.

She opened the door and saw her three dead sons dressed in clean clothes and laid out on the table. Their hair was combed and their hands were folded across their chests. Charley was asleep in the bed, and George sat up with the dead. She walked over and kissed Charley on the forehead and then kissed George. George could tell she was better. He did not know if her mind would ever be all right again. Instead of grief-stricken, she now looked numb. She motioned George out of the chair and she took his place. George crawled in behind Charley in the bed and fell fast asleep.

The next morning, U.S. Marshal Captain W. F. Morton walked toward the door. Behind him were Ranger Augberg and two deputies carrying a large slab of sandstone. Morton had ridden with Forrest in the war and was not a man to be put off. After the war he had taken the oath, and General Forrest's challenge to be good citizens, more literally than most. He had come to Texas and begun marshaling. He even became a Republican, which shocked some people. He thought that if Longstreet could get along with Yankees, then so could he. Besides, the Republicans ran things, and who knew how long that might last?

Collier had disapproved of the whole affair and was convinced that the family would get away. Morton told him, "Mr. Collier, the people of Young County will approve your course in preventing more bloodshed, so take your men away," and Collier did. Morton was not sure what had happened with the whole mess and was determined to clean it up properly and legally. He suspected a mob from the first telegraph he received, and Ranger Augberg concurred once he arrived on site. Now that the Boone boy had shown up poisoned, he felt sure. But that would be left to the courts. He knew Johnson to be an idiot and hoped Collier had a good lawyer. He wanted to warn him but wanted him tried and convicted even more. As far as he could tell, Collier was stupid and was mixed up in somebody else's schemes.

He knocked on the door, and one of the brothers answered. Morton did not have his gun drawn, though he made sure it could be seen on his hip.

"Boys, I have come for you. Give me your guns," he said, calm but determined. George looked tired and was fought out. He did not want his mother to go through another night like that again.

"Can you protect us?" George asked. Morton said he would and walked on past George into the cabin. Once inside, he took off his hat and had the men set the sandstone against the wall outside. He introduced himself to Martha Jane and assured her the boys would be safe in his care. He told her the sandstone slab was for them to inscribe a tombstone for her sons and that several of his men were digging a grave at the Finis cemetery, where Denson had showed them. Martha Jane thanked him quietly and walked outside to look at the slab. Morton was quiet for a moment and then told the boys that they would be leaving as soon as the burial was over. There was no time for coffins; blankets would have to suffice. If there was another mob, they needed to be leaving soon. One of his men was a Methodist lay speaker and duly authorized to perform the service. He said he did not expect any trouble and he did not want to shackle them. He had his men gather up the weapons, and they left the family alone.

As the men left, they saw Martha Jane with a file she had picked up from the yard. She was carving on the sandstone block. The brothers stepped outside to watch. It took a few minutes to see what she was inscribing and it was hardly legible.

ALFRED AND BOONE
AND ELLY MARLOW
WAZ MOBED JANUARY
THE 19TH, 1889 AGE 20
22
24

CHAPTER 21

Charley and George Marlow stood and, like everybody else gathered on the landing, kept their heads turned, looking for the
smokestack of the train. The brothers had hoped all was behind them.
After their siblings were buried properly, they had been taken to
Weatherford, then on to Dallas. That trip they had been well treated
and given a cavalry escort from Fort Richardson when they had to return to Graham for their rustling trial.

The trial had not lasted long. Only one of the Indians had shown,
and he said he had made the whole story up. There remained the
charges of conspiracy that the U.S. marshal in Dallas brought against
several citizens of Graham. The brothers were acquitted of rustling but
ordered to stay in Dallas County until after their testimony as material
witnesses. The Marlows felt otherwise, believing they had performed
their civic duty. They left for Colorado.

The family received irregular telegrams ordering them to return
to Texas, but no legal papers, so they kept about their own business and
began farming in Ouray, Colorado. Denson wrote a few letters. Collier
and Leavell had died in prison awaiting trial, and P. A. Martin had been
released but was not expected to last long, due to the consumption he
acquired in jail. They received a letter from Denson informing them
that the town finally had an honest sheriff and marshal. Johnson was
still lame from his wound and had to be supported by his wife's piano-
lesson money. The final trial resulted in acquittals for most of the mob,
due to the barons' influence and the lack of witnesses. This did not sur-

prise the family. They were glad they had not returned to be witnesses. At least they were still alive.

The brothers were not alone on the platform. Sheriff J. H. Bradley was with them and, at a minimum, they were under his custody—but both Marlows kept their arms. A few days prior, he had arrived at their farm with an extradition request from the governor of Texas for the murder of Sheriff Wallace. Two Texas Rangers were coming to transport them back. Bradley had known the brothers for some while and knew the entire story; he had even deputized them from time to time when he needed extra help.

The brothers had always expected something to go down with Wallace's death. They decided to accompany Bradley and only told their mother it was to help him transport some prisoners. She had her health; her head had never returned all the way. She remained alert—always with a touch of sadness. Both men had married, and she enjoyed being a grandmother. The new Texas governor had been influenced by at least seven of the barons who bonded their men out of jail and convinced the governor to order an indictment of the Marlows, once the mobsters had been acquitted.

Charley mulled over the events in his head as he heard the train whistle a mile away. He thought he should remind the sheriff of George's words when they had met earlier in the week. He walked over to Bradley, who was a friend.

"Like my brother said, we have had a bellyful of Texas justice. We have come to Ridgeway but do not intend to be taken back to Young County under any circumstances. If matters cannot be arranged to prevent it, will you stand aside and let the rangers try to arrest us themselves?"

"Do you know Captain McDonald and Briton?"

"Yes," George replied, annoyed at his brother's rudeness. Bradley was a friend, and there was no reason to treat a friend this way. "We met them in Dallas. They are good men and would be hard to down if it came to battle. They have no doubt made up their minds to take us. But we will no sooner reach Texas than we would be set upon by the same mob that shot our brothers all to pieces, and never live to stand trial. If we have to be killed, let it be here. At least we will receive a decent burial."

The train appeared in sight and prevented Bradley from responding.

He was glad. He did not want to go against the rangers or the brothers and still did not know how he would respond if it came to a fight.

The crowd on the platform had grown in the past few minutes, and parked all around the depot were conveyances of every description. Most were waiting on youths returning from Eastern schools or visits with family. Most were also paper-collars. Colorado had never seen the frontier as Texas and the territories had, and there were already banks and lawyers everywhere.

As the train began braking into its halt, George remembered Charley's favorite game from childhood. They had spent so much time near trains growing up, he had become good at guessing where an engine would stop. Always at a station he would study the approaching train and place his boot down near the edge of the dock. He would then bet his brothers that the train would come to a rest within three feet of his boot, either way. George hoped that Charley would keep his wagers to himself this day.

Before the engine stopped, people inside the coaches began moving toward the doors. The crowd outside did likewise, and soon there was a jumble of people around all the exits. The luggage men could not even get close to begin unloading and stood back until the excitement died away. They held on to their handtrucks and looked bored, unbothered by the crowd.

The jocularity and reunions, the glad-handings and backslappings on the platform had dissipated some by the time Ranger Captain Bill McDonald stepped down from the train. He was tall, taller than they remembered, with a waxed mustache and a healthy crown of gray hair under his hat. His clothes were not those of rugged frontier justice. He was dressed with a fine suit, brogans, and a bowler. He did have on his badge, and anyone could see the hogleg under his sack coat. He waited until his partner joined him, tipped the man for the luggage, and moved off. The brothers made no attempt to catch his eye. They did not have to; he had spotted them from the train window. The two rangers walked calmly over to the men. McDonald appeared friendly, though he was not smiling. The two brothers made sure he saw that they were armed too.

The two lawmen extended left hands to their quarry. McDonald explained that he did not want any trouble. The brothers shook the hands likewise and stated they did not either. The state attorney general had not made his decision yet. Denver was over three hundred miles away, and there was no way to get there by rail from Ridgeway. Bradley had rented a mud wagon and driver to take them by road. He assured them it would only be a few days before they got an audience with the attorney general. McDonald did not look happy. He nodded and gathered his bag and followed the sheriff to the wagon.

The road out of Ridgeway followed the Uncompahgre River for miles. The trip took several days, but the roads were clear and mostly smooth. There was not much talk, and what little there was was overly polite and to the point. Charley and George took turns sleeping so they could watch the Texans. The only time the rangers seemed cautious was at coach stops for fresh horses and meals.

Once in Denver, the brothers slept in a livery while the rangers and Bradley boarded at a hotel across from the capitol. The lawmen were on government per diem and could afford the pleasantries; George and Charley could not. Each night the brothers moved so as not to be kidnapped back to Texas by the rangers. Sleep was better away from the laws. They agreed to meet every morning for breakfast at the hotel, and Bradley vouched for them. McDonald knew he had no say.

After a few days, they finally were seen by the attorney general. He was well aware of the family's story, and several prominent Colorado families had telegrammed the governor's office on their behalf. They were ushered into the main office, and the Texas lawmen noticed it was rather plain compared to the Austin capitol.

The meeting did not take long. After a few minutes they were joined by the attorney general, who made no effort to introduce himself. He spoke quickly and to the point. He regretted that Colorado could not allow any of the Marlow family to be extradited to Texas. There was ample evidence that Wallace was killed by a now-dead brother and that had been an accident anyway. He also expressed his safety concerns if the two brothers were to be in custody in Texas. He read a portion of the telegram the Colorado governor had just dictated to the Texas governor saying as much. He then bid them good day, and another man appeared to usher them out of the office.

The ride to Ridgeway did not seem to take so long. It took a few miles out of Denver for either brother to realize that it was finally over. All the way back, George thought about his dead little brothers, especially Boone. He had been tough on his baby brother his whole life and so dearly regretted it now. Every so often he would think of something funny Boone used to say or do and laugh a bit. Charley would always ask, "What?" And George would just say, "Boone," and then Charley would smile as well.

They arrived in Ridgeway and overnighted again and waited with the rangers for their train the next morning. Before boarding, McDonald stuck out his right hand to both the men. They took it and returned his smile. He said he wished them good luck and prosperity in their lives. George and Charley said they would sure try.

—◆—

Oscar G. Denson poured out some of his canteen on his hankerchief, then used it to daub his forehead. He felt like an old man who had spent too much time behind a plow. August was the last month of summer and the worst, as far as he was concerned. The last few days had not been prosperous at all. His mule had thrown a shoe, and his plow blades needed sharpening. He had hoped both would last until the work was finished. He could not afford to pay for their mending. He had tried shoeing before and either wound up getting kicked or laming the animal. He finished the cool rag and tried to think through how to pay for both. At least he did not need any more seed.

He had waited on the porch of the "old Marlow place" all morning. It was neither old nor the Marlows', except for a few months in the fall and winter of '88–89. The place had stood vacant since then. Denson often thought about moving in himself. They had no children and were too old to even think about it now, and their other house was too big. Besides, the outbuildings were better down here, and access to the fields was closer by at least a mile. He had not seen the Marlow family in over two years, though he tried to write them as news happened. He owed them a letter soon. A fellow was supposed to be here any minute to discuss renting the cabin; maybe that would work out and he could tell the Marlows about it. Not to mention having some greenbacks to shoe the dray and fix the plow. If the fellow did not show up soon, Denson would get back to work. But he needed the money and had grown comfortable with the idea of a boarder for the income, at least.

Denson wet his kerchief down again and tied it loosely around his neck. He needed to get back to work. This fella was not going to show. Just then, Denson spotted a rider turning into the road. Maybe that was him. Denson waved and began walking out toward the main road. The man was not dressed like he could afford a room, much less a house. Denson scolded himself for being judgmental. Fellow looked like a drover, maybe was tired of hiring out and had saved some cash back and wanted to run his own cows. Maybe he could shoe as well. Probably had lots of money, just did not like to waste it on clothes. He had a decent horse and probably a fine saddle.

The rider reined up as Denson joined him on the road.

"Hidy," Denson said and stuck out his hand. The rider did not offer his. He was dressed like it was January. A mackinaw, hat pulled down. All bundled up.

"Are you Denson?" The man asked.

"Yes, sir. Are you here about renting the cabin?"

"No. I am here about vengence." And the man pulled a twelve-inch coach gun from inside his coat and shot Oscar G. Denson in the head with both barrels.

⊷⬦⊶

The metronome continued to click. Sometimes, when it clicked in time with the second hand of the clock on the bedroom wall, it was not so bad. But today his wife's piano pupil was especially stupid and could play, if it could be called that, at only the most mongoloid pace. Former deputy U.S. marshal Ed Johnson was sure the sound would eventually drive him to insanity. There was no asylum in Young County, and they would probably have to ship him north to Wichita Falls or east to Dallas. He worried about that. What the clicking and his wife's clucking did not finish of his faculties, the several-day journey in a buckboard no doubt would. He would probably have to be restrained, at least bound by the legs. With one arm and a useless hand, he could only kick someone a few times before he lost his balance and probably could not run far either. Johnson allowed himself a smile, then noticed the clicking again, then the clock.

Over the years he had lamented Wallace's death, yet was grateful the man could not see him like this; two useless appendages, and he had to be helped to eat, shave, drink, scratch, dress, and wipe the scat from his arse. The only thing he could still function himself was making water; of course, he had to squat like a woman to do that.

He half listened as his wife admonished her student again, for not practicing enough or some such dung. He was sorry he had ever met her. Were it not for her musical tutorial skills, he would have starved or been institutionalized years ago. Her music lessons were their only income now. They had once lived in a medium-sized cottage, not far from his old office, that had been paid in full by the barons. That was gone, and they now managed in a small two-room just off the square.

At first the barons had wanted him dead for his treason against them. They had Denson killed for it. Few knew that Denson was a member of the Cattleman's Association. The barons remembered and took care of him. Johnson worried he had the same thing coming. After all, he was the one who made wise the federal judge to the scheme. The Marlows were acquitted, the bastard Harmonson was killed, and Collier and Leavell rotted to death in prison. The barons eventually recovered and managed to divert all attention and blame to Collier and the mobsters. The only regret he had, aside from losing an arm to Frank James, getting his one good hand shot nearly off, and meeting his wife, was in not killing Harmonson and Collier himself. That would have been a fond memory to reflect on. Both of them shot to pieces and begging for mercy or perhaps a cool drink of water. Life was such a disapointment.

When his wife initially nursed him, he used to wake in a nightmare that she had gone and left him alone. Now it was like a fantasy. He had another. If he only had one good hand, he would blow his own brains out. He would wait for just the right time, while his wife was at church for instance. Then he would go and sit on the stinking swivel stool she had ordered from the Sears & Roebuck catalog, turn his back to the piano, put the pistol in his mouth, and shoot the back of his head off. All over the piano. That was what he would do if he had one good hand left.

EPILOGUE

So much of history does not lend itself to novels. Novels must condense, highlight, and in certain cases exaggerate historical facts in order to weave a story. Hopefully, not too much of that has gone on in *A Pilgrim Shadow.*

The story recounted is true and occurred, more or less, as depicted. Certain liberties were taken, events and characters consolidated to weave details of a better narrative. For example: George Marlow was accused of stealing an Indian's horse while at Fort Sill, but it happened several years prior, and historically there was no Young County connection. Still, it needed to be told and provided an excellent springboard for the telegram to Johnson. A sheriff in Colorado sent the original telegram. Why a Colorado sheriff would send a telegram to a federal officer in Texas concerning rustling in the Indian Territory remains a mystery. For purposes of a fictional retelling of the Marlows, it did not fit. So the Fort Sill horse incident was moved forward, and Agent White's role was expanded to form the catalyst. For purposes of this narrative, these liberties were rarely taken.

With few exceptions, the Marlow family has been presented, both in life and death, as it was. A notable omission were the wives of George, Charley, and Alf: Emma Copenbarger, Zenia Davis, and Lillian Berry, respectively. These brave frontier spouses stood with their husbands throughout the ordeal. However, I wanted Martha Jane to rise as the matriarch alone on the frontier with five sons and believed she would be better served as a solitary female figure. The brothers remain at rest in the Finis cemetery today. The pathetic tombstone was hand-carved by Martha Jane along with the boys' wives. It was removed in the late 1990s by the modern Marlow family and placed in the Marlow Museum in Marlow, Oklahoma.

The anti-Marlow mob in Graham presented its own problems. There were at least two dozen men involved in this persecution, too many for a novel. The characters of Harmonson and Martin, though not fictitious creations, represent the consolidation of all these hooligans. I chose to let the barons remain anonymous, and though Jeffery's was a saloon on the north side of the Graham square, the back room and its skullduggery are purely elements of my imagination.

As much as possible and where known, the participants' actual conversations have been woven into the story. These were drawn from historical record in various published sources, most notably the titles listed on page 149. Nineteenth-century language was more colorful, melodramatic, and formal than that of the twentieth century. Additionally, to remain loyal to these people and their time, I have used their vernacular as much as practicable. People of the trail normally said "hoss" instead of "horse." I have tried to use this as a seasoning to flavor the narrative and trust that it does not confuse many readers.

Graham has been remarkably unblemished by progress. The county jail is still there, in the modern guise of a late-twentieth-century "Bible Church," though the second floor has long since been removed. The federal courthouse is now a restaurant, but Judge McCormick's home remains much as it was. Jeffery's and the town of Finis (except for the cemetery) are all gone. In Oklahoma, Fort Sill and the Comanche Reservation still stand as monuments to both justice and injustice. The town of Marlow, Oklahoma, exists in the rough vicinity of the Wild Horse Creek property of the Marlows. There is a small museum that contains one of the sad, bloody shackles removed from either Elly or Alf. The town of Marlow hosts a reunion for the clan every fall, called "Outlaw Days." The Young County Museum at Fort Belknap has some mementos as well, most notably the red and black checked sack suit (complete with bullet holes and blood stains) and hat worn by Frank Harmonson that night at Dry Creek.

The family finished their days in Colorado and California. Martha Jane lived a decent life surrounded by her grandchildren from both Charley and George. George Marlow even tried to enlist as a truck driver in World War I. Charley died 19 January 1941 from influenza. George passed four years later on 3 July of heart failure; he was eighty-nine years old. Whenever he was questioned about the family's struggle in Graham, George would respond, "I love everybody. I ain't got an enemy in the world. But I'd go a hundred miles to shoot at a mob."

FURTHER READING AND ACKNOWLEDGMENTS

For further reading on the Marlows, the following books are recommended:

Ledbetter, Barbara A. Neal. *Marlow Brothers' Ordeal, 1888–1892: 138 Days of Hell in Graham on the Texas Frontier.* Graham, Texas: Privately published by the author, 1991.

Rathmell, William, ed. *Life of the Marlows: A True Story of Frontier Life of Early Days, As Related by Themselves.* Ouray, Colorado: Ouray Herald Print, W. S. Olexa, publisher, 1928.

Shirley, Glenn. *The Fighting Marlows: Men Who Wouldn't be Lynched.* Fort Worth, Texas: TCU Press, 1994

Elohim Adonai receives all credit and glory for this work. I would like to thank the following for their assistance, counsel, and help with this novel: Steve Abolt, Angela Buckley, Fred Chiaventone, Jim Donovan, Ed Eakin, Mike Enger, Amber Forgey, Steve Hardin, Steve Harrigan, Mickey Hoy, Paul Hutton, Bert Kalinsky, Mike Kalinsky, Barbara Ledbetter, Lisa McCool, Russ McGee, Virginia Messer, Debbe Ridley, Marlene Rodgers, Barbara Sanford, Mickey Shapiro, Amber Stanfield, Bill Stone, Virginia Thomas, Tammy Valentine, Gail Young, and Scott Zesch. Any and all literary or historical problems are the sole responsibility of the author.

About The Author

Alan C. Huffines is an eighth-generation Texan, Persian Gulf veteran, and active-duty combat arms officer. He is the author of *Blood of Noble Men: The Alamo Siege and Battle, an Illustrated History*, and has been a Selected Author of the Texas Book Festival. He was also featured on C-SPAN's "Book TV." He holds both a BA and an MA in history and has been published in various historical periodicals.

Huffines is a member of the Company of Military Historians, the Texas State Historical Association, and the Western Writers of America. He and his wife, the former Caroline Cotham, have three daughters and make their home in Central Texas.